FRAME
Shop

Critiquing another

writer can be murder.

Donald J. Bingle

This book is published by

54°40' Orphyte, Inc.
St. Charles, Illinois

ISBN 13: 978-0692342626

ISBN: 0692342621

November 2014

10 9 8 7 6 5 4 3 2 1

Please consider writing an honest, thoughtful
review of this publication.

Novels by Donald J. Bingle

Forced Conversion
GREENSWORD: A Tale of Extreme Global Warming
Net Impact

Stories and Story Collections by Donald J. Bingle

Writer on Demand™ Vol. 1, Tales of Gamers
and Gaming
Writer on Demand™ Vol. 2, Tales of Humorous Horror
Writer on Demand™ Vol. 3, Tales Out of Time
Writer on Demand™ Vol. 4, Grim, Fair e-Tales
Writer on Demand™ Vol. 5, Tales of an Altered Past
Powered by Romance, Horror, and Steam
Writer on Demand™ Vol. 6, Not-So-Heroic Fantasy
Writer on Demand™ Vol. 7, Shadow Realities
Crimson Life/Crimson Death
Season's Critiquings
Gentlemanly Horrors of Mine Alone
Running Free: A Tale Inspired by Patsy Ann
Father's Day Deluxe 3-Pack

Also from 54°40' Orphyte, Inc.

Ratfish by Buck Hanno
Surrounded by Love: A Story of Orphans
and Family by Marjorie L. Bingle

For all of the members,
past, present, and future,
of the Gen Con Writer's Symposium,
Origins Game Fair Library, and
St. Charles Writers' Group.
Sorry, but this dedication page
and the acknowledgments section
are the only places in which
any of you appear in this book.

Table of Contents

Prologue 1
Chapter 1 9
Chapter 2 19
Chapter 3 23
Chapter 4 31
Chapter 5 41
Chapter 6 49
Chapter 7 55
Chapter 8 63
Chapter 9 69
Chapter 10 83
Chapter 11 93
Chapter 12 101
Chapter 13 111
Chapter 14 119
Chapter 15 125
Chapter 16 131
Chapter 17 139
Chapter 18 147
Chapter 19 153
Epilogue 163
Addendum 167
Acknowledgments 173

FRAME
Shop

Prologue

Guy stifled a yawn.

The image was strikingly clear to his eyes, sharp as the knife itself. He saw it in high definition and slo-mo, the drops of cherry-pie red blood being flung from the flanks of the tungsten-sharp blade and spraying in lines and arcs across the too clean, short-pile, white rug, the flat-white plaster walls, and the overstuffed starkness of the chic, white, sectional sofa of the Scandinavian-featured, young, professional woman who was the recipient of the repeated thrusts.

The woman, delicate, pale, and white before the attack, was whiter now than her monochromatic decorating, any color she once had having been transferred thrust by thrust by frenzied thrust onto the furniture, walls, and even the ceiling.

White was never good for funerals and this was hers.

Her feeble struggles had long ago ceased—it took only one practiced, forceful puncture to kill a person—but her body continued to absorb the fury of the violent assault as her open, blue eyes stared disapprovingly at the increasingly garish splatterings of blood around the 2,500 square foot, tastefully modern, high-rise box that had once contained her pristine, white life.

Guy laughed, not the laugh of a psychotic maniac, but the gruff, low bark of a professional killer critiquing a crime scene. The sequence of events that had led to the once-fetching, young woman's demise was improbably fortuitous.

Why had she let the cabbie drop her off at the side of the building, instead of the well-maintained circular drive at the front door of the tony complex?

Why had she made a leggy, brief dash for the elevator without watching to see that the building's side door had latched behind her?

Why, oh why, had she held the elevator door from closing so her killer could ride up in the car beside her, smiling unabashedly as he appraised her figure up and down, like an express elevator stopping only at the locations of greatest interest?

Why had she failed to even attempt to punch the alarm button—right next to the open door button she had punched so adroitly only moments before—as her attacker lunged at her, forcing her into the corner of the tiny, rising box as he felt her up crudely?

Why had she failed to scream as he strong-armed her down the hallway to her door and forced her trembling hand to turn the key and let them both in, bolting the door behind them? Dead-bolting the door.

But, for God's sake, why did she then, finally and stupidly decide to show some misguided, Swedish chutzpah by insulting his manhood, pointing and laughing *after* he had pulled the knife?

Stupid move. She died of stupidity, the victim of a violent, senseless crime.

The killing made no sense and it was taking forever. Worse than a director's cut, this was an overly-indulgent director's cutting frenzy.

At least the knife was sensible. Wicked sharp, with a very large hilt—essential to protect the hand from slipping down onto the blade and being cut as the knife plunged again and again into the increasingly pliable, wet, sticky chum that was once somebody's daughter ... somebody's lover ... somebody's life. Yet, Guy didn't know her name and didn't care. The brand name of the knife was more important to him than her name. It was a damn fine knife.

Guy couldn't hear the wet shuck of the stabs or the gurgling, sucking sound of the dagger being removed from the bloody bosom of the victim. He had never heard her feeble protests, nor even the "ding" of the elevator door. He had seen, but not heard, her derisive laugh.

It was silent in his world, but he saw everything.

Despite the grisly scene being played out before him, Guy couldn't help but let loose his yawn. He stood in the bushes, watching, waiting ...

... waiting for his target to shut off the lousy flick on the damn television.

A wide-screen set didn't do a thing to improve a production as bad as this one, though the crisp definition of blood droplets did give a new meaning to the phrase plasma television. Still, his target stared at the flat panel of vivid color without emotion, mesmerized by the ersatz violence and frenetic chase scenes.

Would the bad-movie buff ever go to bed? Oh well. At least his target wasn't watching porn—not that this slasher movie crap had much more in the way of plot—but Guy had no taste for standing here in the bushes biding his time until a balding, overweight, fifty year-old got his rocks off.

Guy disliked waiting, but he had his rules, his *modus operandi.* All professionals did. He almost never hit someone at their own house when they were awake. A target had too many advantages in his own home; he knew where the phones were, where the weapons were, where the exits and hiding places were. No, he would wait until the target turned off the wide-screen, plasma monitor and went to bed, then wait fifteen to twenty minutes after the light turned off in the master bath. Most people fell asleep within seven minutes after going to bed, especially late at night, but Guy always liked to give them a little time to really zonk out.

He had already taken his usual pre-hit precautions. It took only a minute or two to locate the NID—an amateur would call the network interface device a phone box—behind some bushes along the side of the house. As was usually the case, it was unlocked. A quick scan showed there were no impediments to simply unplugging the house's two phone lines from their connection to the main line. That, in turn, would effectively disable the crappy mass-market security system. Oh, some stupid alarm noise might trip on as he entered the house to rush toward the bedroom, but he didn't care about that—not in a neighborhood with estate-sized lots. What mattered was whether the system could automatically call the alarm company, which would call the cops in a few minutes, but not until after checking for a false alarm by phoning for a code word. Thousands of dollars for sensors and keypads and relays and it could all be defeated by unplugging the fucking phone lines outside of the house. People had more money than brains, that's for sure.

He didn't unplug the lines, though, not yet. The target might try to make a call to his wife at her sister's place in San Bernardino or for a pizza or, God help him, to some 900 number sex-chat line. Instead, Guy stood next to the NID, concealed by the overgrown bushes, watching *Psycho Maniac Killer 4: The Body Count Rises* from a distance through the dining room windows, biding his time, and waiting to do his job. He didn't begrudge the time, even though he obviously wasn't paid by the hour. He just found the whole thing boring.

Hey, it was just a job. He wouldn't do it if they didn't pay him, that's for sure. It's not that he had moral compunctions or that it was overly unpleasant—usually it was just two shots in the back of the head, the victim's bowels sometimes loosing before the shot, always after—but there was the chance of getting caught. And spending time in prison was like standing here in the bushes waiting for his life to continue, except there was no high-definition screen, no CineMax, no apartment and girlfriend to go back to afterwards, and the wait lasted twenty years to life.

Yeah, getting caught would suck.

The really irksome thing was that, besides being boring, jobs like this no longer really paid as well as they once did, as well as they should. There were too many punks, gangs, and druggies undercutting the market, too many do-it-yourselfers, and too many eager up-and-comers willing to off someone for free—for free!—just to impress the boss. He sighed. Oh well, he was too old to change careers now.

Finally, the credits rolled and his target scratched his belly for a second as he stood, then thumbed the power button on the remote. The crisp scrolling of the forgettable names that worked so industriously to produce a forgettable movie starring forgettable actors coalesced into a dull, silver luminescence for a few moments before winking out altogether. Guy rolled his shoulders minutely to work out any stiffness from his wait and glanced at the dial of his watch. Twenty minutes and counting. The jerk had twenty minutes left to live and he had no fucking clue it was going to be the last twenty minutes of his life.

Worse yet, he had just spent his last two hours watching *Psycho Maniac Killer 4: The Body Count Rises.* Was that sad, or what?

#

Less than an hour later, it was over.

Two in the back of the head with a .22 caliber, just like always. The bullets didn't have enough velocity to exit the skull once they entered. They just ricocheted around inside the brain case, turning the mind to mush without creating much of a mess to clean up.

One less viewer for *Psycho Maniac Killer 5.*

Guy drove more than forty miles from the scene before picking up a Bacon, Egg, and Cheese Bagel and a Diet Coke at an early-opening Mickey D's and dumping his rubber gloves along with the paper refuse from his meal into a trash barrel in the parking lot. Fast food places were very prompt about their trash pick-ups—that piece of evidence would be compacted before ten a.m. and on its way to the dump before noon.

He didn't need to call his employer to report the job was done. There would be a story in the papers in the next day or two, no doubt. Presumably the fellow could read. He didn't know his employer's name anyhow; everything was done through a friend of a friend of a friend in this business. All he knew about the man who put out the contract was that he made enough money to afford Guy's fee. And, unless you were a rap star or a unionized garbage-man, that kind of dough usually meant you knew how to read. Besides, calling in the kill, even if he knew who to call, was just one more way to leave an evidence trail and get caught.

Guy didn't want to get caught.

Maybe he would go shopping for a new knife on his way home—that knife had been the highlight of his evening. One hell of a product placement, that. The guy in marketing who had arranged the use of the knife in the movie had done a fine job for his employer.

He wondered if the marketing guy read the newspaper stories about stabbings, looking for a mention of the brand of knife. He was probably disappointed if he did. Newspapers never mentioned that kind of technical detail. Information withheld to help the cops eliminate or confirm suspects, no doubt. But if the papers ever did mention the brand or he tuned in to Court TV, where all the real stuff of trials actually got shown, would the adman get a warm feeling of self-satisfaction or a vicarious thrill of excitement? Or did he just think of it dispassionately, as a job well done? It was a job that would never win him a pat on the back from the boss or the admiration of his wife. It was a job he could have some pride in, just not one he could ever tell anyone about.

Just like Guy.

Maybe everyone's lonely in their job ... in their life.

Chapter 1

Harold J. Ackerman eased his twelve-year-old Honda Civic into a space near the door at the Township Center at 8:54 a.m. He felt his lip curl just slightly as he shoved the gearshift into "Park" and turned off the engine. He was the first to arrive, as usual. Although the Pleasant Meadow Writers' Guild and Critiquing Society met every Saturday at 9:00 a.m., his fellow writers were less punctual—quite frankly, less considerate—than he. Mumbling unpleasantries about them to himself, he crossed the concrete sidewalk in front of the hash-marked handicap zone in the empty parking lot and stepped into the utilitarian landscaping surrounding the government building. Squatting, he retrieved the Township's spare key from its hiding place under the third paving stone leading from the outdoor hose bib to the sidewalk.

Shaking off a few pieces of damp cedar chips from his shoes, he unlocked the doors and entered the building. Stale, warm air greeted him. He rebuffed the assault by adjusting the air conditioning, then rearranged the chairs and tables still set up from last Thursday evening's Township Board meeting into a rectangle suitable for participants to write, whilst still being able to all see one another. The rest of the PMWGCS would straggle in over the next twenty minutes, gossiping and socializing and generally being of as little help to him as they were in the critique sessions that occurred at each meeting. Still, as a pillar of his local community and a professional writer, it was his civic and authorial duty to attend each and every meeting of the PMWGCS and pass on his wisdom to the amateur wannabes and assorted poseurs who made up the bulk of the organization.

"Good morning, Harold," chimed Felicity Morton, as she bustled her way to the middle chair of the narrow end of the rectangle farthest from the door. She set down an unwieldy pile of manuscripts, reference tomes, literary magazines, poetry chapbooks, and assorted tea bags. "Oh, dear. You haven't started up the hot water yet." She waddled her middle-aged, overly plump frame toward the kitchenette counter on the right side of the main meeting room. "I don't know how anyone expects to start on time if things aren't set up properly."

Harold pushed his reading glasses up with an extended middle finger as he feigned forcing a condescending smile in her general direction. "Perhaps, if I had some assistance ..."

"Hackerman, dude," bellowed an unkempt grad student as he bounded in the door with the lithe grace of youth. "A cat mystery? Really? I gave up reading Thoreau, so I could comment on a cat mystery?" He plopped down into the chair closest to the door. "That's lame, even for you, Hackerman."

Harold did his best to disintegrate his youthful, overly exuberant critic with an icy glare. "I've asked you not to call me that, Bryce. It's both inaccurate and disrespectful. This is supposed to be a collegial gathering of fellow writers assisting one another with encouragement and specific criticisms sandwiched between sincere dollops of praise, not a mean-spirited ambush of slash and burn attackers. I can get that kind of writing critique with an internet group."

Bryce flashed a smile, before contorting his toothy grin into the most insincere attempt at faux sincerity Harold had ever witnessed. "I have no doubt at all you could, Hack. No doubt at all."

Harold bit back a response as the others of their weekly group arrived and took up their usual positions. Besides Felicity and Bryce, all four of the other regulars were in attendance: Sandra, who insisted everyone call her "Minx," was, as usual, dressed entirely in leathers which Harold imagined (vividly) came from an S&M shop, with the piercings and Goth make-up attendant thereto; Carl, a crusty nonagenarian who wrote lusty memoirs about the action he'd seen during World War II; Myrtle, a middle-aged *haus frau* who was 278,000 words into an epic fantasy about the life and loves of a huge, unpronounceably-named cast of dragonfly-mounted faeries; and Bob, a beat poet with exceptionally poor rhyming skills and worse hygiene.

"Now, now, children. Settle down," cooed Felicity. "We've lots of work to do."

"I'll say," murmured Bryce.

Felicity's eyes flicked toward Bryce, somehow turning menacingly dark for an instant, like the eyes of monsters in cheesy horror flicks. "Any announcements? Any successes?"

Harold's hand shot into the air.

"No need to raise your hand, Harold. We've been through this before. It's a small group. We're all friends here."

Bryce coughed.

Harold ignored both Felicity's admonition and Bryce's surprisingly healthy-sounding cough. "Yes, Felicity. I just wanted to announce I've been published yet again. This time by *The New Yorker.*"

"*The New Yorker!*" exclaimed a voice with a slight Southern twang from behind Harold, at the doorway to the Township Hall. "This is an impressive writing group."

Harold turned in his chair so he could stare, along with the rest of the PMWGCS members, at the interloping arrival.

The fit-looking man standing at the door was dressed in surprisingly crisp jeans and a fashionably-logoed golf shirt. Both his full, lush, brown hair and his uniform nails looked as if they had recently been professionally trimmed. "Gantry Ellis," said the man to the group with a nod of greeting. He turned his head slightly as the door thumped shut behind him and fixed his politician-quality smile on Harold. "Poetry? Short story? Don't tell me you're a cartoonist ..."

Bryce harrumphed. "Another letter to the editor, no doubt. As if that counts as publishing."

Harold spun his head and gave Bryce a hard stare. "Millions of people will read my words in *The New Yorker*. Real authors are read. That's the definition of being published. The cumulative audience for your epic poem about the Civil War is ... a half-dozen so far. Most likely less—Myrtle's yet to make a substantive comment on it, so I suspect she gave up somewhere in the morass of stanzas about the political precursors to the war."

"Oh, my," whispered Myrtle, as she looked down at the table.

"Now, now," asserted Felicity. "Let's all behave. We critique writing here, we don't attack other authors."

"Authors?" smirked Bryce.

Felicity turned up her smile and made a show of ignoring Bryce and focusing on the new arrival. "Please have a seat and tell us about yourself. Then we can all introduce ourselves."

"Thank you kindly," replied the stranger as he moved to a chair on the kitchenette side of the rectangle. "Much obliged." He reached into a fashionable leather valise and pulled out a small stack of light-gray papers. "As I mentioned, my name is Gantry Ellis, but I write under the name Cain Abel ..."

Harold could hardly contain himself. "THE Cain Abel, the author of the Danger McAdams mystery thrillers? I downloaded all six of them to my Kindle this past year. Read each one of 'em in a single sitting." He didn't bother to mention he had gotten all six of the thrillers for free during various promotional periods—why spend 99 cents or, heaven forbid, $4.99 a clip if you didn't have to?

Gantry chuckled. "There's no 'The' at the front of my pen name. Just 'Cain Abel,' and, yep, I've had a bit of success with a few tales." He handed the stack of papers to Harold—it was a writing résumé on thick, luxurious stationery, with a color photo and an impressive listing of publications. "I thought this would let you all know what I've been up to, writing wise."

There was a minor hubbub as the papers were passed about and admired. Harold noticed the women of the group were all eyeballing the résumé, then the newcomer, in turn, the way he checked out Minx when she wasn't looking his direction.

"Imagine," gushed Myrtle, "a real, live publishing legend in our little group. My name is Myrtle—I'm close to halfway through a high fantasy novel. Nothing as commercial as your work, I'm sure."

"Now, Miss Myrtle," replied Gantry—the twang just a tad more noticeable as he addressed her—"I hear that Tolkien feller, he did alright with his story of orcs and dragons and such. I'm sure you'll do right good with it, once it's finished." He smiled at Myrtle, who had gone beet red, then adjusted his gaze to the next individual.

"Harold J. Ackerman. Fellow mystery writer, with a background in journalism."

Bryce interrupted: "You delivered newspapers as a kid?"

"A degree in journalism, I'll have you know. From Wakefield College." Harold found himself straightening his posture as he spoke.

"You sure you didn't leave off the word 'Junior' from that last sentence *fragment?*"

"Now, now, boys," admonished Felicity. "Never mock education. It's the bedrock on which all writing is based." She turned back toward Gantry. "Wouldn't you say so, Mr. Ellis?"

"Tis a wise person who values knowledge, ma'am," replied Gantry. "Hard enough these days to find someone who reads the newspaper, much less someone professionally trained to write for them."

Gantry turned to the next person.

"Bryce Hannigan." Bryce nodded in greeting. "Epic poetry, as you heard." He chuckled. "As Hack ... er ... Harold has already noted, my writings have absolutely no commercial potential whatsoever. I'm afraid no one's made a go out of epic poetry since Homer, but I don't mind."

Gantry returned the nod. "Always happy to meet a gentleman and a scholar, Mr. Hannigan."

Carl saluted Gantry from his seat. "Carl Pilkington, Sergeant, United States Marine Corps, Retired. Sorry not to stand, but, well, I'm old enough to remember Homer ..."

The group chuckled.

Pilkington's bright eyes moved with an alacrity his body no longer could manage, fixing each one of them in turn with a steely gaze. "Not personally, you nincompoops. I mean I remember Homer from school, back when they still taught the classics and students paid attention."

"I understood your meaning from the start, sir. May I thank you for your service to our country and venture the opinion that if you had known Homer when you were both in your prime, you could have taken him in a fair fight."

"Fair fight, my ass. Only purpose of a fight is to win. I would have thrown sand in his eyes and stuffed pebbles in his sandals when he wasn't looking, son. But nice to meet a young feller who admires the classics, like me." He winked at Gantry. "Punctuate that remark any way you like."

Gantry shifted his gaze to Minx.

"I'm Minx." She shrugged. "Semi-autobiographical ruminations and dark prose poetry. Kind of a dialogue of the disillusioned, I guess." She shrugged again. "Hey, there."

"I look forward to reading your dialogue."

Bob sniffed, stepping on the auditory end of Gantry's sentence. "Given name's Bob, but my stage name is Steely Slash Rab ..."

"It is?" murmured Bryce under his breath.

Harold rolled his eyes. "This week, I guess."

Bob ... er ... Steely Slash Rab stopped speaking abruptly and looked long and hard, first at Bryce, then at Harold, before continuing. "I give voice to the common man over the tumult of the mass media corporate conglomerates and their constant, dinning refrain of 'buy, buy, buy, until you die, then fork over your savings so in a grave you can lie.'" Steely Slash Rab glared at Gantry in defiance.

"Er, right on, brother ..." replied Gantry, seeming somewhat taken aback for the first time since entering the writers' conclave. "Organ donor ... then cremation, myself." Gantry's eyes darted about, as if seeking assistance. "Word."

Felicity filled the awkward silence. "I'm Felicity, and I'm kind of the Emily Dickenson of the group." Harold stifled a scoff. Well, Emily Dickenson in the sense that Felicity was female, mostly unpublished, and fond of the wonders of nature. A more accurate description would be that Felicity was a perpetual contributor of meandering slice-of-life musings about nature to obscure literary magazines and an occasional submitter of mushy familial sentiments to greeting card companies. "Well, then, Mr. Ellis ..."

"Gantry, please, ma'am."

Felicity blushed. "Well, then, Gantry. Here's how this works. We have a brief period for announcements, encouragement, and the like, then we verbally critique the materials we each handed in to the group last session, then turn over the paper copies on which we may have made additional remarks, like editing, word choice, and typo comments not worthy of bringing up during the discussion. At the end of the session, we pass around the materials we each brought to be critiqued for the next session." She glared in the direction of Bryce and Harold. "Despite some inappropriate comments by a few of our members this morning, our goal is to provide meaningful, constructive criticism, sandwiched in between layers of compliments and encouragement. Helpful support, that's our motto here. Helpful support."

"Just what I'm looking for," replied Gantry. "You just go ahead and get started. Pay no nevermind to me. I'll just listen in for today's session."

Chapter 2

The only thing that kept Harold from leaving—from marching out of the PMWGCS in a huff—during the critique of his latest story was that they did his critique last. It wouldn't look like he was genuinely hurt by their reactions to his story, which ranged from boredom to scathing sarcasm; it would simply look like he was leaving early because the arrival of a new member had made them run late.

Besides, he had to lock up.

So, instead of walking out on the motley crew of wannabes and poseurs, he gritted his teeth as the critique droned on.

"I just don't get it," complained Bryce. "Why would anyone write a story about a cat solving crimes? I don't think guys are looking for this ... genre ... when they Google 'mysterious pussies.'"

"Now, Bryce," admonished Felicity, "we are not here to criticize the subject of the writing, but to help with the effectiveness of the writing, itself."

"Besides," murmured Myrtle, "Barnes & Noble put out a whole one-hundred story anthology of nothing but cat mysteries. It's an established niche market."

Bryce held up his hands in apparent surrender. "Fine, fine. Let's put myself in the mindset of the typical consumer of cat mysteries. I'm sure I can stifle my sense of taste and lower my IQ for a few moments." He looked down at the pages and quickly looked up again. "The mystery isn't really all that mysterious. I mean, the banter between the detective cat and the witness is cute in a kind of 'Kitten of the Day' website way, I guess. But the whole angle of the story is a reveal. Am I right?"

Harold said nothing.

Felicity spoke up again. "You know the author isn't allowed to speak during the critique, Bryce."

"Fine," said Bryce with an exaggerated eye-roll. "Does everyone here agree the 'plot arc' of this ... story ... is nothing but a reveal that the detective and the witness are really cats?" He looked around the group while Harold clenched his jaw even harder. "Anyone?"

Myrtle, Felicity, and Carl gave cursory nods. Minx simply looked down at her copy of the story and turned the pages, as if looking for an answer or, possibly, reading the tale for the first time. Bob leaned back in his chair, scowling as if such proletariat issues as reveals or cats were world-wearying and mundane. Gantry flipped through a spare copy at a rapid clip, his eyes tracking quickly and professionally over the words.

Bryce nodded his head with vigor. "I'll take that as a 'yes.'" He looked over at Harold. "I know you can't talk now, Hack, for which I'm, believe me, eternally grateful, but if I'm wrong, just ... blink twice or something." He turned away from Harold without waiting for a response, as if Harold would engage in such petty foolishness.

Bryce continued. "But, here's the thing, people ... it's a story written for a niche market of cat mystery anthologies! Isn't everyone who reads it ... say, both of Hack's parents ... already going to know the characters are cats? If so, what's the reveal? What's the fucking point?"

"Language ..." muttered Myrtle. "There's no reason to curse."

"Don't forget the sandwich critique method," reminded Felicity.

Bryce looked over at Myrtle, apparently chastened. "I'm sorry, Myrtle. My bad. Skip the 'fucking.' There's simply no point to this cat tale of any kind whatsoever." His eyes flicked over to Felicity, then to

Harold. "But the letters are nice and dark and crisp against the white paper, Hack. Gotta give it to you, you don't skimp on the toner."

Bob ... er, Steely Slash Rab ... gave Bryce a 'ba-da-bum' rim shot with his hands on the hard plastic tabletop.

Harold teetered on the edge of a pithy response, if only he could think of one, when Gantry interrupted.

"Pardon me for cutting in here, you all, but I think you're being a mite hard on Harold, here. I mean, cat mysteries may not be my cup of sassafras, but the mystery/thriller market, she's mighty fragmented. Who-dunnits. procedurals ... y'know how-dunnits ... action chases, cozies, accidental detectives, true crime, paranormal mysteries, zombie detectives, political thrillers, romantic mysteries, psychics, gorefests, and scifi Holmes ripoffs, just to name a few. I git that you're not the target demographic for this little cat mystery, here, but it's got a place. Writing's clear, dialogue snappy with a side of cute, from what I can tell on a quick pass. Can't make a living on this kind of stuff, but it's nothing to be ashamed of."

Harold sat in stunned silence. Cain Abel, a *New York Times* bestselling author, had lavishly praised his mystery. Maybe he should ask for a blurb.

"Any other comments?" cooed Felicity, looking about. "Harold, anything you'd like to say about the critique."

"Uh ... uh ... no. I mean, thank you," Harold could barely breathe. His head swam. He turned toward Gantry ... the legendary Cain Abel. "Thank you."

The PMWGCS had just taken a turn for the better.   Suddenly, Harold knew this was his chance to really show off his skills and get the break he always craved, the break he always deserved.

Chapter 3

Six sessions later, Harold was not so sure his initial assessment had been right. Oh, Gantry continued to attend and it was exciting to read snippets of action scenes and interrogations of thugs and killers by Danger McAdams, scenes which the series' hungry fans had not yet seen, but nothing had really changed. At their quarterly group reading, Bryce had thundered out the last three stanzas of his epic poem in *basso profundo*, Minx had whispered her way through a darkly disturbing prose poem about ritualistic cutting, Myrtle had spent five minutes describing a nymph in such abundantly purple prose that Harold had briefly dozed off, and the others had likewise done their usual thing.

Finally, it was Gantry's turn.

The bestselling author ambled his way forward to the podium Harold had set up for their reading session.

"This is from my latest work in progress: *Danger Ahead.*"

#

Danger rolled to his right and spat blood from his split lip onto the coarse brick of the tenement flanking the alley—that would give something for the Crime Scene guys to do—then pulled his feet under him and elbowed his way to a sitting position before standing with a guttural grunt, making sure not to use the brick wall for support as he rose. If you started using support to get to a standing position, you were too old to be a private dick anymore. That, or you were on the losing side of the fight. The sprawled corpse of Dmitri Natakowicz stumbling-distance away testified Danger hadn't lost the fight, though he'd taken damage along the way.

Never bring fists to a knife fight.

Of course, the knife protruding from Dmitri's left eye proved you shouldn't bring a knife to a knife fight if you didn't know how to hang on to it when using it against a middle-aged brawler with a survival instinct and a mean right hook.

Danger staggered a few feet to an old-fashioned metal garbage can covered with a dented lid and half-sat on it to catch his breath and sort his thoughts before the cops arrived. Without thinking, he fished an unfiltered Camel out of the crumpled pack in the pocket of his torn and filthy sports coat and thumbed his disposable Bic to light up. He enjoyed a good smoke after a fight. The nicotine calmed him and the need to take a long drag regulated his ragged breathing. Besides, there was something strangely life-affirming in doing something dirty and disgusting and disapproved of by society when you were savoring the outcome of a fight to the death.

His tongue flicked a few tendrils of tobacco off the end of the cigarette, tucking them into the corner of his mouth next to his still bleeding lip, anesthetizing the inner surface of the wound and spreading a sweet, oaky flavor along his tongue just before he inhaled the smoke deep into his lungs, casually holding it a moment before exhaling through his nose so as to spread his vice throughout his respiratory system as thoroughly as possible. He wasn't half-assed about his faults. He fought hard, drank hard, and smoked hard. As far as he was concerned, all three were requirements of the job.

He wasn't an idiot. He knew smoking kills—drinking, too. But there was no doubt in his mind that fighting would kill him first, so nothing else scared him.

As always, the distant wail of the first siren reminded him of Connie, screaming as she fell from the bridge, the torn cuff of her lapel clutched in his outstretched hand, but he shook it off. Best not to live in the past. Nothing ever changes there, especially your regrets.

He took a big drag from the Camel, sucking in all of the savory death he could, then let the cig dangle from his swollen lips as the first squad car squealed to a halt at the end of the alley. He calmly raised both hands, not because he was a bad guy, but because he didn't want to die. Cops looking into a dark alleyway and seeing a dead body can make stupid mistakes out of fear and he didn't want to ruin a cop's life by being an innocent victim of a bad shoot.

Besides, he still hadn't rescued Angela. A dead bad guy didn't mean the case was solved, just that there was no one to torture for information. Next time, he'd try to stab the bad guy in the cheek, instead.

Nah, that wouldn't work; the guy wouldn't be able to talk and he might keep fighting. Better to go for the groin—painful, lots of blood, and humiliating. That would be a much smarter move.

One cop cuffed him as the other covered him, both hands gripping his service revolver at arm's length. Definitely a rookie. Danger remained placid during the procedure, focusing on fixing the groin-knifing move in his mind. He filed the action away for future need with all the other desperate techniques in his repertoire of dirty tricks, so it would pop into his head automatically the next time his best lead in a case ambushed him.

Long-term strategy was the first thing to go in a fist-fight to the death. You had to think out how to be nasty ahead of time if you really wanted to be a bad-ass in a fight. And nice guys, they always finished last in a fight.

Heck, by his reckoning, only half the bad-asses walked away.

The cops took away his cigarette stub and tossed it into a nearby puddle as they walked him toward the squad car. He ducked his head when entering without being prompted. He knew the routine. Like fighting and death, getting arrested was just part of his job. He hadn't learned that on Career Day. No, he had the scars and the rap sheet to prove it.

Two hours. Three tops, and he'd be back on the streets busting heads and asking questions. He hoped Angela was either already dead or unconscious. He didn't want her to suffer because of any delay caused by offing one of her kidnappers.

#

Gantry nodded once at his fellow writers, then folded the loose pages he had been reading from and ambled back to his seat. As he did, the group burst into applause, none clapping more enthusiastically than Harold, himself.

As the meeting began to break up, Harold ignored his usual clean-up responsibilities and positioned himself between Gantry and the door. As the bestselling author approached, Harold moved toward him, extending one arm for a handshake and quickly wrapping the other around the big guy's shoulders.

"Nice scene, Gantry," he gushed. "It's so good to finally have another author in the group who understands suspense and tension and pacing in their work. Even your internalizations have a gritty action feel to them, a kind of hyper-realism."

Gantry gave Harold's hand a brief, firm shake and kept moving toward the door. "Well, to get into the mindset of a character like Danger doesn't just take imagination. You have to research the field, get to understand what private detectives do day in and day out, then jettison the boring parts and ramp up the action and the description."

Harold saw his opportunity. "I understand completely. I'm a journalist, as well as a writer, as you may recall. I know you have to sort through a lot of information to get at the salient details. If there is anything, anything, I can do to help out ..."

"Hackerman, dude! You're blocking the door." Bryce made a shooing motion with his hands as he approached. "Suck up on your on time, bro. Epic poet coming through."

Harold felt his blood pressure rising, which meant his face was undoubtedly reddening, too. Not the impression he wanted to make on Gantry.

Gantry pivoted a quarter-turn and took two steps back. With his arm still around the author's shoulders, Harold had to step quickly to maintain his position vis-a-vis his conversational target, half-stumbling in the process, but Gantry didn't seem to notice. Instead, his attention was focused on Bryce.

"Now, Bryce," drawled Gantry, "you'd think an epic poet would know the value of an occasional pause ..."

Bryce chuckled. "Well, I guess if I brake for animals, I can stop walking for a moment to avoid a collision with a writer of cat mysteries."

" ... and journalist," interjected Harold.

Gantry nodded. "You don't want to collide with a member of the press. They control the news, you know." He turned his head and gave Harold a hard look. "We'll step aside. I've got something I need to chat about with Mr. Ackerman."

He did? Harold barely perceived the rest of the group cleaning up and filing out into the sunshine. Gantry Ellis, the man behind Cain Abel, the author of the Danger McAdams series, wanted to chat with him. This was his big break. Maybe he needed a co-author—it had to be hard, cranking out a new mystery every six months. He knew some of the big-time scribes merely outlined plots and let others do the fleshing out of their stories. Some seemed to simply add their name to works primarily penned by others. Heck, he wasn't sure when Tom Clancy had last actually written something on his own, and James Patterson seemed to have his name on a new book every month. What percentage of the royalties should he ask for? I mean, Cain Abel's marketing muscle was critical, but he would actually be doing all the heavy lifting ...

Suddenly, Harold realized that everyone else was gone and Gantry was talking to him.

" ... need someone to conduct a research interview for me, or at least go to meet the guy and see if he shows."

Huh?

Harold scrunched up his eyes for a moment. He always imagined the act not only focused his attention, but somehow squeezed blood out of his forehead deeper into his skull, improving the flow into his brain, making it ... him ... sharper, more alert.

"Why wouldn't an interview subject show up? What did he say when you set up the appointment?"

Gantry's left hand fluttered. "It's not like that. This guy is a contact of a friend of a friend of a source I used for background material on my fourth Danger McAdams book. That's how this business works."

"Writing?"

"No," replied Gantry, scrunching up his own face for a moment. "Killing. Like I said, this guy is supposedly a professional hit man. You don't just call a professional killer on the phone and schedule an interview. It's all very circuitous. I asked my source if he knew any pros I could chat with and he said he'd ask around and, you know, three weeks later I meet my source for coffee and he says this guy he knows

knows a guy who knows a guy who is a pro and he says to meet him at a time and place and maybe he'll be there, if I come alone, and maybe he'll talk if he doesn't get a weird vibe."

"So, why don't you want to go? Bad neighborhood?"

Gantry shrugged. "Sure, it's a bad neighborhood. These guys don't hang around suburban libraries and such. Bad neighborhoods are great, 'cause the locals always have an eye out for cops and such. It's like an early warning device for busts and sting operations. But that's not why I'm not going. It's just that it's a long shot and a time consuming one at that and I'm on deadline for the paperback galley revisions for my last book, *Danger Untold*."

"So you want me to go on a wild goose chase." Harold realized as soon as he said it that this wasn't the right way to respond to his big break ... not that it really sounded like much of a big break. "I mean, not that I'm not happy to ... take the meeting for you." After all, he knew, you have to crawl before you can walk and, he guessed, you had to work your way into the inner circle of a bestselling author by doing a bit of drudge work.

"Glad to hear it," replied Gantry. "I can't just send anybody, you know. If he shows, I need to have someone with interviewing chops. And knowing the kind of details a writer would want to know is pretty important, too. And you, Harold, you just seemed like the ideal person to help me out."

"Happy to help."

"And, of course, I'll pay you for your services. Say, twenty bucks an hour, including travel, plus a mention in the acknowledgements if the guy shows up and gives you anything I end up using in the book."

If there was anything Harold liked more than the idea of being a writer, it was the idea of being paid for being a writer. Maybe he could parlay a mention in the acknowledgements of a Danger McAdams book into an entrée for getting an agent.

He reached out his hand once again, this time to shake the hand of his partner in crime-writing. "It's a deal. But, won't this guy be expecting you?"

Gantry laughed. "He doesn't know squat about me, just like I don't know squat about him. That's the nature of a clandestine meeting. No names, no nothing. My guy said to just show up and see what happens next." Gantry winked at Harold. "After all, that's what readers do every time they open a book. They want to see what happens next. We'll just have to turn the page and find out, just like them."

Chapter 4

Guy scanned the Mexican restaurant, but found no threats. He sighed and rolled his eyes. What the hell was he doing here? Not only were the warped linoleum floor tiles the same sickly yellow as the stack of broken and cracked taco shells at the end of the self-serve counter, but the faded posters promising an all-you-can-eat taco bar for $2.89 did not inspire confidence in the quality or sourcing of the ingredients. Come to think, he hadn't heard a single dog or seen a single rat on the three-block walk here from the subway stop. Coincidence? He thought not.

He sipped at his cup of hot tea to quell any rebellion from his stomach at the smells of the place. Assuming they weren't washing the cups in piss, there wasn't a lot you could do to mess up hot tea. Nothing to it but water hot enough to kill most germs while it scalded the skin off the roof of your mouth, plus a tea bag produced in conditions more sterile than this place had ever seen. At least he hoped the tea leaves got washed at some point; he'd never seen a picture of rural China with a Port-A-Potty near the fields.

No, the tea was fine, but that didn't explain what the hell he was doing here. It could be a set-up, cops holed up in the kitchen waiting to pounce, maybe a bug hidden under the table to record some confession or incriminating fact. And there was no way he was getting on his hands and knees on this floor to look at whatever crap might be under the table—boogers and gum would be the least of it.

The meet was risky and unpleasant. And for what? Just because his friend, Mook, said the whole thing was for an author friend of a friend who wanted to talk to a professional hitter? Was his life so boring, was he so hard-up for thrills he would risk getting arrested just so he could talk about his work with somebody who might appreciate the effort and skills he brought to the table, even a table with chipped Formica and a surface as dull as the personality he maintained to stay under the radar? A low profile with a side of dull was good when not only the cops were looking for you, but so were bad guys out for revenge.

One thing for sure, as soon as this "author" showed up, the two of them were getting up and going elsewhere for their chat. This place gave him the heebie-jeebies and that wasn't good for his safety or his professional image.

He looked out the greasy, smeared window and saw the dweeb author even before he walked in the door. Everything about the fellow gave him away: the prissy Police Benevolent Association sticker on the bumper of the ancient Civic; the inability to properly parallel park the car in a space big enough for an old Buick; the nervous twitching as he fumbled his keys to open the trunk and get out a small stack of notebooks and a clunky cassette tape recorder; the repetitive head swivels as the geek checked out whether he was being followed; the careful checking of the address of the Mexican restaurant against an index card produced from the rear pocket of his Dockers; and the plaid sweater vest. Definitely the plaid sweater vest.

As the geek timidly opened the door and stepped into the place, Guy stood up, flipped a five onto the cracked Formica table-booth and strode toward the entrance.

"Yeah, I'm the guy you're here to meet. Shut up and turn around. We're going for a walk."

Guy thought he heard the sweater-vested dweeb yelp as Guy grabbed his elbow and spun him a hundred and eighty degrees and propelled him out the door, where the sour smells of the inner city improved upon the stale stench of the restaurant.

"Um ... er ... What do you think you're doing?" squeaked Sweater Vest. "Where are we going?"

"Nowhere I'm gonna say out loud, at least until I check you for a wire." Guy continued to bum rush Sweater Vest down the street. "Just shut up 'til I say so. Understood?"

"Uh ... yes."

Guy growled. "Next time just nod."

Sweater Vest nodded. Guy smiled. People in his profession liked to be in control. He was comfortable he could control Sweater Vest.

Sweater Vest was a good boy for the next fifteen minutes, saying nothing and doing what he was told as Guy kept up a brisk walk, scooting in and out of alleys and making plenty of detours on his way to a neighborhood park, stopping en route between two large garbage bins in one of the narrower alleys while Guy did a thorough frisk for wires and weapons. Sweater Vest even managed to hold it together without a peep, though his eyes went wide, when Guy felt up his crotch. Guy knew a competitor who always hid a Danish hand grenade nested between his balls under a foam rubber jock strap, just in case he ever got into a really bad situation. The cops, they were always delicate about searching there, whether due to homophobia or respect for privacy, Guy didn't give a damn. It was the best place to hide something you didn't want found if you were pretty sure there wasn't going to be a strip search.

Sweater Vest opened his mouth as if to protest when Guy tossed the cassette recorder into one of the dumpsters, but then just pressed his lips firmly together and followed along.

Guy still wasn't sure why he'd agreed to this meet, but as long as he had, he wasn't going to be stupid about it.

They got to the park and Guy steered them away from the benches—too easy to bug and too frequented by people just standing or sitting around. Instead he began to simply stroll along the running track, as if they were cardiovascular workout buddies rehabilitating after a heart attack.

No other runners or joggers, not at eleven in the morning on a weekday.

"So, you just here to chat about the trade or is this an elaborate set-up cuz you're looking to hire?"

Sweater Vest paled. "Just here to talk. I don't want anyone ..."

Guy interrupted before Sweater Vest could say something direct and incriminating. "... inconvenienced. You don't want anyone inconvenienced."

Sweater Vest only looked confused for a split second, then he furrowed his brow and nodded gravely. "Yes. I mean, no. I don't want anyone inconvenienced."

"Good. Cuz I never deal direct on matters of convenience."

"So you're the guy, the guy who does the 'inconveniencing.'"

What the hell was he doing? Sweater Vest had seen him, could describe him, could probably lead the cops to a dumpster with an old cassette recorder with his damn fingerprints on it. He froze for a moment, unwilling to compound his stupidity by actually confessing to something, anything.

"No," he finally said. "I'm not that guy. You don't understand. Nobody's that guy. Nobody you ever talk to, nobody you ever see, is that guy. He's invisible, unapproachable, unidentifiable. He's hypothetical."

Sweater Vest seemed to catch on. "So, there's this hypothetical guy who does the inconveniencing?"

"Yeah. That's right. A completely hypothetical guy."

"But you, you're close to this hypothetical guy? You can tell me all about him, all about how one goes about inconveniencing their fellow man."

Guy pondered a moment. "I can tell you what he tells me, this hypothetical guy. Can't say whether it's true or he's just a good liar, like you writer types."

Sweater Vest smiled at that before responding, like lying was a compliment. Maybe he had a day job as a lawyer.

"So, hypothetically speaking, what do I call this guy?"

Guy laughed. "Call him Guy, cuz, you see, he doesn't have a name. He doesn't have an address. He's just a guy somebody who's friends with someone else knows. That's the way the business works." He gestured with his hands palms up as they continued to stroll the running path. "Or, so I'm told."

"But, you can answer my questions, right?"

"Shoot."

Sweater Vest flinched at the word, but quickly stammered his way to what passed for composure. "So, what's it like? You know, killing people."

Guy closed his eyes so Sweater Vest didn't see them roll. "Jeez, you're not one of those types, are you?"

His companion looked around, as if to see what type Guy was talking about. "Er ... What type?"

"Somebody who gets their jollies imagining what it's like to control life and death, spending all day thinking about how they might do it, how hot the arterial spray from a severed head is ... all that psycho shit."

"No, no, nothing like that." Sweater Vest broke out into a sweat. "Is arterial spray really hot?"

"Ninety-eight point six degrees, Sherlock. What do you think a thermometer is measuring when Mommy takes your temperature?"

"Oh," said Sweater Vest. "I guess that makes sense."

"Yeah, well if you want more of that kind of crap, you should go find a serial killer, not a hit man ... I mean, friend of a hit man. Hitters, they're not in it for the passion. They're in it for the money ... mostly cuz it pays well for a limited amount of effort and they don't have too many other remunerative job skills."

Sweater Vest took a couple of quick steps to keep up with Guy's walking pace. "Sure. I can see that. That's the kind of insight that will be useful, you know, in my book."

"Great, but time's wastin' here, so ask what you need to ask so I can be on my way."

"Well, why don't you start by telling me how someone gets into the business?"

"Hell, getting into this job is just like getting into most any job kids never dream about when they're young. It's not something you plan for and map out. You just kind of fall into it, gradual like. You run with the wrong crowd, you get into a few fights as a juvie, you help out a friend who needs a driver or a lookout for a small-time job. You spend too much time workin' out to impress some stuck-up princess you got the hots for and you get a reputation as a tough guy cuz you don't let no one push you around. Pretty soon, some hood on the up and come, he tags you to stand around and look menacing when he's shakin' down the bodega owners and newsstands in the neighborhood for protection. Someone doesn't pay and you rough 'em up and maybe things go too far, or maybe someone asks you to make sure things go too far, and the guy dies." He stopped walking for a moment and leaned in closer. When the dweeb did the same, Guy looked him straight in the eye. "But here's the thing, when that happens, you don't let it get to you. You don't freak out, you don't go cryin' to your momma, and you don't look over your shoulder any more than everyone does regular. You just treat it as another piece of your business."

He paused for a moment and thought back on his life. "That happens a couple 'o times and you doin' nothing noticeable in response, that gets you noticed by the people you work for and the next time they have a sensitive situation to deal with, they think of you and approach you to do the deed." He started walking again.

Sweater Vest scrambled to catch up. "So, you just start doing jobs on the side, like people write on the side, until the income stream becomes big enough and dependable enough you can quit your day job."

Guy couldn't help but notice Sweater Vest straining to equate their positions. The dweeb flushed with excitement, like a gawky kid on his first prom date anticipating a little under-the-bra action.

Guy scrunched up his nose while he thought how to best respond. "Don't know much about writing. All them complicated plots on the TV mysteries make my head spin—whackin' people is usually a whole lot more straightforward than that. Nah, after the first couple of jobs, you either make the leap straight to full-time hitter or you end up a bodyguard or a street brawler or maybe a smash-and-grab guy."

Sweater Vest frowned. "Why's that? Why do you have to make the jump to doing it full time?"

Guy snorted. "Survival instincts. The clients who want you to do jobs for them, they don't want you doin' other crimes, cuz you might get pinched and roll on them for some murder when you were looking to beat five to ten on some home invasion or something. And you need to keep a low profile, you know, criminally. The cops gotta stop thinking of you when they think of potential perps in the neighborhood. So, if you're smart and are thinkin' ahead about your career, you take the payoff from your first couple of jobs and you use it to get a place somewhere quiet and bland outside of the neighborhood."

Sweater Vest furrowed his eyebrows. "You mean, like the suburbs."

Guy laughed. "Not that fucking quiet. And, I ain't picking up a wife and kids just for show—too expensive and too high maintenance. Besides, you don't want anybody too close that can flip on you or fuck up any alibi you might need to fake. Nah, someplace in the city, just some place nicer than here." He thought for a moment about how much he was willing to reveal. He could go a bit further yet.

"Apartment buildings with a lot of divorced guys are good. Nobody thinks it's weird that you're livin' alone or that you disappear for days or weeks at a time. They don't care if you have different dames to the apartment, even pros, but they don't freak out if you don't neither."

Guy could see the kid kinda half-smiling, like he was describing nirvana, instead of some bland apartment in a building full of guys using too much Rogaine and too much Viagra in an attempt to capture the virility of their days as a single guy on the prowl.

Damn, it was good to be able to talk to someone about his life.

He wasn't stupid, though. He chatted for a bit more, then cut the interview off.

Sweater Vest looked devastated. "But ... but, I've got more questions."

"A guy's gotta be careful ... even when he's just talking hypothetically about somebody he might or might not know in the business."

Jeez, he hoped the kid wasn't gonna cry.

"Look," he said, partly to forestall any expression of emotion from his interviewer. "Let's just let the dust settle. When and if I feel comfortable ... and my hypothetical friend feels comfortable ... we can meet and chat again, here in the park."

Sweater Vest perked up. "That would be great." Suddenly he frowned. "But how will you contact me?"

Guy chuckled. "In the old days, I would've placed a classified ad in the local daily newspaper. Now? I'll advertise an All-Star Program from last year on Craigslist and include the hit, run, and error stats for the game in the ad. That way, you'll know it's me."

"So, then I call you?"

Guy narrowed his eyes. "Hell, no. The phone number will be a fake—some random digits. Just come by the park the following week on Tuesday, at 11 a.m. You'll either find me or some instructions taped under the bench over there." He nodded toward a standard green park bench between two overgrown bushes. "If a month goes by and you don't see the ad, don't ever expect to see it or me again and don't come lookin'. You understand?"

Sweater Vest nodded nervously.

"Good. Take a seat and get some rest. You don't leave this park 'til I'm gone a half hour. Are we clear?"

Sweater Vest nodded again. "Good-bye."

Guy gave him a squint-eyed look. "Nobody says 'good-bye' in this racket, except with a bullet."

Chapter 5

Harold did what he was told, spending the half hour—almost an hour, in fact—thinking about the interview, committing the details to memory to be able to write them down fully. But the more he thought about the interview and the prospect of more interviews to come, the more he decided not to do what he was told. At least, not what he was told to do by Gantry Ellis. He didn't want to be an errand boy, passing on details like this to Gantry, when he could write them up himself, make up his own story about a hit man, and propel himself to the top of the charts. Maybe not a *New York Times* bestseller, but, at least, on the more mainstream *USA Today* bestseller list.

No. He'd simply tell Gantry the guy was a no-show, pocket Gantry's twenty dollars an hour for his time, and keep this Guy character all to himself. What could possibly go wrong?

#

Gantry seemed disappointed, but not terribly surprised, by Harold's report.

"Why do you think he didn't show?" asked Harold, doing his best to play the scene as he would have written it.

Gantry wrinkled his nose. "Hard to say. Criminals are a skittish bunch. Might have just not felt right come the day." He shrugged his shoulders. "Or he just may have slept late 'cause he was carousing the night before. We'll never know and, frankly, it doesn't matter."

Harold nodded in agreement.

Gantry continued. "Sorry to waste your time, but I appreciate the help."

Harold shrugged his shoulders back at Gantry. A lot of Harold's characters shrugged their shoulders—he found it to be a very useful, all-purpose, show-not-tell gesture. Eye-rolling was good, too. Bryce criticized him constantly for overuse of both gestures. Whatever, he turned his attention back to Gantry. "Got paid to drive into the city and soak up some atmosphere in a crappy part of town. I've got no complaints. Whatever doesn't kill you makes you a better writer."

Gantry tilted his head and gave Harold a hard stare, then shook it off. "I guess that's one way of looking at it."

That day's writers' group was a blur to Harold. He couldn't wait to get home and check Craigslist for the hundredth time. Maybe today would be the day.

#

That Saturday wasn't the day, but it did come, almost two weeks later. Harold jumped up and pumped his fist when he saw the ad, as if he'd gotten a passable review on Goodreads.

Harold knew the drill for this next visit. No recording devices, wear comfortable walking shoes, etc. He planned out his questions and committed them to memory. This was his big break and he wasn't about to mess it up. He'd keep going on the general, background kind of stuff first, until his subject became more comfortable with him and more relaxed and unguarded in his statements. Then he'd get more specific, more personal, and get the real dirt, the kind of nitty-gritty detail that would make Gantry Ellis gasp, and get Harold a starred review on all the big websites.

It took four sessions for that moment to come.

#

Guy took a liking to Sweater Vest. Everyone likes to have a fan after all. And the kid, he seemed to hang on every word Guy said. It was nice to be able to talk to someone about his work. Still, he was careful. He tried not to say anything that could come back to haunt him or identify him to the authorities. He also threw in stuff from other hits he knew about just to mix things up, even crap he had read in those pulpy, hard-boiled detective books he used to filch from his dad's bedroom closet when he was a little kid. He needed to satisfy Sweater Vest's craving for detail, while making sure that, if the kid talked to anybody, he would end up looking like an idiot. Guy had no intention of getting caught, but setting up his interviewer for impeachment as a witness in some future trial was just smart contingency planning, and any good hitter made plans for when things went wrong.

Still, he was more relaxed talking to Sweater Vest than he was talking to everyone else—even hookers, who generally assumed anything you told them was a lie, whether you said "I've never done this before" or "the girls, they usually pay me" or "I'm just out of prison, where I killed a man for looking at me wrong." The whole profession of hooking was built on lies, on both sides of the sweaty sheets.

They were walking, this time at the dilapidated zoo near downtown, as they talked. There was a lull in the conversation after Guy had explained to Sweater Vest what kind of knife was best for a quick, silent kill, when, suddenly, the kid got way too personal way too quick.

"So, tell me about your m.o., your average day on the job, so to speak."

Guy stopped short. "Are you fuckin' crazy? You want to know my m.o.?

Sweater Vest stopped, too. "Uh ... yes ... That means your *modus operandi.* It's Latin. It means your typical method of operation on a hit."

Guy gritted his teeth and managed not to backhand his interviewer or stalk off without another word. "I know m.o. means *modus operandi.* And I probably know more Latin than you. Masses were in Latin when I was a kid, you know." Fuck. Why did he let slip he was raised Catholic? Anonymity was everything in this biz.

Sweater Vest seemed more excited today than at their last session, as if something was going down. He had developed a Nixonian upper lip sweat sheen, the type that had gotten the first and last Catholic president elected. "Then, what is the problem? If you knew what I meant, why'd you get pissed?"

"First off, asshole, I don't have an m.o. My hypothetical friend, he has an m.o. And second, you don't ask about a hitter's m.o. You think he's gonna reveal a detail that's gonna get him connected to every job he's ever done?"

"Oh."

"Yeah. Oh. You see, if a guy is gonna do this and do it professionally, he's gotta think ahead. Time, place, potential problems, potential witnesses, escape routes. All that shit. A standard m.o. is handy cuz it limits down the variables. Like two from a .22 in the back of the head, for instance. That lessens the chance of blood spatter, because the muzzle velocity of a small caliber bullet ain't sufficient to penetrate something as thick as the skull of a target more than once, so the bullet goes in, but it don't come out. It just bounces around, turning the target's brain into canned cat food mush. And that means greater certainty of a quick death. No time for screams or calls for help or any of that shit."

Sweater Vest looked as if the cat food reference had made him a bit queasy. Licking his lips across his salty upper lip probably didn't help. "But doesn't that mean the cops recover the slugs?"

Give the kid points. At least *his* brains weren't cat food. "Now you're thinking. Good question. But, y'see, a .22 tends to get pretty fucked up, itself, bouncin' around. Besides, .22s are cheap as shit. You can get a new one every job—just a cost of doing business, if you know what I mean."

"So, then, it's smart to do that all the time, right? That's a good m.o. for you ... I mean for the guy you know."

Guy turned and started walking down the exercise path once again. "Sure, yeah. I suppose it could be," he lied. "But a standard m.o. has a downside, too. It links all the jobs to each other, backwards and forwards. And that ain't good. The cops, they may not know who the hitter is, but they know it's the same guy, so they call their friends at the NSA and subpoena records from the world wide interwebs and crap and they try to figure out who they suspect might be in the 'inconveniencing' business coulda been all those places all those times. You do enough jobs, you know, and that begins to weigh on your mind ... at least so my friend says ... and sooner or later you begin to think there might be a better way, but then you're old and set in your routines and you ain't got enough imagination to do anything else, you know?"

"You could just change your m.o., couldn't you? Use pills or poison or a garrote or something different, to throw off the authorities. Make them not realize that all the murders were linked, maybe lead them away from murder or at least toward a different suspect. Someone not in the business, like, say, a loved one or business associate."

Guy snorted hard and then spat, not on the walk, but in the grass where the snot would be difficult to spot or retrieve should anyone be watching. "Sure, you could do that. But that takes a lot of research. Not just on methods of killing, but on who could be credibly framed. I ain't got the time or proclivity for that shit. Besides, the CSI types, if they get any whiff you might be involved, they seize every piece of electronics you ever touched and sort through your porn to see what sites you visited and what crime shows you watched and all that crap. That's a finger pointin' right at you. And no librarian is gonna look up that stuff for you."

Sweater Vest shrugged. "You could say you were a writer. I look up things like that all the time. You know, for my stories. The FBI and the NSA and the CIA and Homeland Security, they probably all know I've spent hours researching undetectable poisons and countries without extradition treaties and how to fire a surface-to-air missile, but they don't care, 'cause if they know that much about me, they also know I'm a writer."

Guy ran his tongue across his teeth. Jesus, this yokel was depressing him. It was like putting a bunch of fancy jewels in a display case with bright lights, but having a sensor on the glass and an armed guard standing right there. Tantalizing shit, but no way he could get his hands on it. He gave a low chuckle to jolly himself out of his mood. "Yeah, well, I ain't no writer. Ask Mrs. Wachowski, from the fourth grade. My penmanship sucks and my spelling is for shit."

Damn. Why had he used Mrs. Wachowski's name? "But I guess they do have that Auto-Spelling-Check crap or whatever now, right?"

Sweater Vest sniffed and straightened his posture somewhat, even as they continued to stroll down the exercise path. "Real writers don't use spell-check or grammar check. Besides, spelling and grammar, those are the easy parts. Writing is hard work and not just the technical stuff. Plotting is hard work, too. You've gotta figure out credible motivations for the characters, understand their backstory and what makes them act the way they do. You also gotta know how to construct a timeline—how long everything takes and who is where when. Then you've gotta put it together in a way that directs the story where you want it to go, that lets the reader come to the conclusions you want them to, without ever realizing you're manipulating them. It's not as simple as those the-characters-tell-me-what-they-want-to-do-next assholes make you think. That kind of attitude disrespects the craft, the work, the talent of a true writer. You can't fake real writing."

Guy shrugged. The kid was probably right. "If only I could outsource the storyline of the job, you know, the motives, methods, and means of misdirection, to a real writer-type. You know, somebody who could research the information I need. Give me a script to follow. But they have no connection to the crime or the location or the business, so they aren't ever the subject of investigation."

Maybe the screenwriter for *Psycho Maniac Killer 4: The Body Count Rises*. The fellow did know his fucking knives, even if his plan of attack did depend on a lot of serendipitous coincidences. But even if he knew the screenwriter's name, how could one go about approaching someone like that? It was fraught with danger, just like when people were looking for a hitter like him. There were too many ways things could go wrong and someone could rat you out. That's why all his jobs came from friends of friends of friends, not from cold calls.

Fuck. Who did he know that was a writer? Who did he know who was a writer who somebody he trusted had vouched for?

Oh.

He was staring right at him. And he was wearing a god-awful, ugly-ass sweater vest.

Chapter 6

Harold could almost see the gears turning in the head of his walking companion, thinking it through, coming to the logical conclusion that he, smarter by far than this cloddish thug, had already come to. Finally, he could hold his tongue no longer and simply blurted it out.

"You mean, someone like me? Someone who's a real writer?"

That's what he was, after all. A real writer. Just like Gantry Ellis. Someone who researched facts and studied places and things and understood the motivations of characters and could keep multiple timelines straight and plant false clues and red herrings and plot his way out of a locked room mystery and not only make sense of it all, but write it down in a clever and cogent and accurate way so even a cloddish thug like this guy ... or this guy's friend ... could follow the path he steered them onto.

"Sure," said his contact. "Someone like you. Someone who was willing to put in the time, research the situation, and construct a plot for a story that would only ever be read by one person, though the condensed version might end up in the papers or the courts someday." His companion stopped walking once again and turned to him, jabbing with his finger as he spoke in a low voice. "Someone who is a friend of a friend, who can be trusted, and who would be well paid for his effort and his ... discretion."

Harold almost peed himself. Not just a writer, but a paid ... a very well paid ... writer. He did his best to be nonchalant. "Why don't you talk to your friend and see if he's looking to hire? Commissioned works are always better for a writer than spec work. The payout is certain because the customer has asked for exactly what they want."

"Is that so?"

"Suicide, accidental overdose, crime of passion, mugging gone wrong, whatever. I can give your friend exactly what he needs."

Harold couldn't believe he had mustered the courage to be so assertive. It must be the adrenaline coursing through his veins because of the whole cloak and dagger nature of the meet.

He choked back the Humphrey Bogart accent that had begun to creep into his voice, unbidden. "For the right price, of course."

His contact wrinkled his brow. "I'll meet you on the bench, right over there, a week from Tuesday, 2:22 in the afternoon. Sharp. I'll talk to my hypothetical friend and see if he has a hypothetical work of fiction he is interested in reading."

Here's looking at you, kid! Harold wanted to jump for joy. Instead, he stayed in character. "Understood."

His companion walked away, leaving Harold behind, in shock. He could scarcely believe it. Truth was stranger than fiction.

#

"Are you sure this is fiction?" asked Bryce, as the PMWGCS took up Minx's latest submission, a prose poem about sexual assault and abuse. "Because, if it's not, you need to involve the police."

Hack could barely keep himself from rolling his eyes. Bryce could be such a drama queen, always being so didactic, whether it be about grammar, meter, or how other people should conduct themselves.

"If you're afraid to call them," the epic poet continued, "just say the word and I'll call them for you."

"Oh, dear," murmured Myrtle.

Felicity spoke up. "You know she can't talk, Bryce. The author is not allowed to talk during their critiques. It keeps people from becoming defensive; it prevents arguments."

Bryce shot Felicity a scathing look, all furrowed brow and slitted eyes. "I think we can make an exception for criminal activity. Don't you?"

Carl joined the verbal fray. "If you don't want to involve the police, just give me a name and address, Minx, and I'll take care of the bugger. Men these days, they don't know how to treat a lady." He rapped his cane hard against the flat of the table. "Hell's bells, when I'm through with him, he'll be a lady."

Minx looked down at the table, her shoulders hunching, her back slumping, as if she wanted to fold in on herself and disappear.

"Now, now, gentlemen," huffed Felicity. "No bullying of the author. Sandwich critique method ..."

"Shut up, Felicity," growled Bryce. "Criminal activity exception. During the duration of a criminal activity exception, no one gets to speak *but* the author. Understood?" He turned back toward Minx. "Well?"

"I ... I ... was just trying to make my writing more visceral. Bob ..."

"Steely Slash Rab," interjected Bob.

"Er ... Steely Slash Rab wrote on my last submission that my language wasn't gritty enough ... that it lacked emotional realism."

Bryce tilted his head to one side and scrunched up his nose. "You're sure that's it? You're sure none of this really happened."

"Man," interrupted Steely Slash Rab, "don't you understand? Things like this happen all the time. You ... all of you ... are just blinded by crass materialism from understanding what is really going on in the world."

Bryce shot Steely Slash Rab the kind of glare he usually reserved for gratuitous adverbs. "Shut up, *Bob*. I'm talking to Minx. I need to know the character talking isn't her. It is written in first person, after all."

Minx squirmed in her chair. "It's just writing. It's not real. Nothing's real. I'm not real."

The group was silent for a few moments. Finally, Felicity took charge once more. "Does anyone else have anything to say about Minx's piece?"

Harold cleared his throat. Finally, the faux drama had passed and they could get down to serious business. "Despite the fact that publishers constantly recommend writers learn the lessons of Strunk & White's *Elements of Style*, the author omits serial commas on pages three, eight, and nine."

"Anyone else?" chirped Felicity, who waited barely a moment before continuing. "Minx? Any response to the group's comments? Now is your time to talk."

"Uh, no. I mean, thank you for your comments and ... uh ... caring enough to take the time to comment ... to say what you said."

Gantry spoke up in a clear loud voice. "That's what we're here for, darlin'. We're a support group. We're here to support *you*, not just your writing. We're your friends. Heck, some people say I'm a good writer, but I'd much rather be known as a good friend." He looked around the room. "I'd say that goes for all of us. Right?"

Everyone mumbled "That's right." Harold joined in, not so much because he believed in Gantry's cornpone sentiments, but because he still had the hots for Minx and maybe he could upgrade from friend status if he played his cards right. Based on her previous semi-autobiographical submissions, she obviously wasn't too picky about who she went out with. He was certainly a more appealing prospect than some unemployed motorcycle mechanic, garage band bassist, or understudy stunt knight for The Medieval Times restaurant off the interstate.

Harold barely paid any mind to the scattered, desultory comments about his essay railing about the ridiculousness of small-print disclaimers at the bottom of television commercials. Maybe the other members of the PMWGCS were as distracted about the exchange with Minx as Harold was distracted by his upcoming meeting with Guy. Most of the critiques of his essay were mechanical and technical, though Bryce said the piece was "the most commercial thing" Harold had ever written. Gantry suggested re-titling the piece "Attempt This," which was clever.

Attempt this.

It was more than clever. It was a sign.

Chapter 7

"I don't know if I should be doing this," Guy growled as he sat down on the bench next to Sweater Vest.

"Doing what?" replied his colleague ... his partner in crime ... his fucking co-conspirator, as he looked up all sweet and innocent and sweater-vestery.

"Shut up," Guy barked as he stood back up. "Let's walk while we talk."

Sweater Vest got up and followed docilely as they made their way to the walking path. They'd walked less than fifty yards down the path before the geek couldn't contain himself anymore. "So," he said, leaning in close, "what's the job?"

Jesus, this dweeb made him paranoid. "I thought I told you to shut up."

Sweater Vest skipped a step, so the two of them were walking in sync. "I thought you said we were going to talk while we walked."

Guy looked around the park. Nobody around. Another half hour before school was out; the morning and lunchtime runners were long gone. If this geek was undercover, he was flying solo. Even with a code word, he had no hope of back-up reaching him before Guy ganked him, if he wanted to do something so garish and impulsive in such an open setting.

Still, he had to be sure. "Lift up your shirt ... your sweater vest and your shirt. One at a time."

"What?"

"You got five seconds or this meeting is over."

Sweater Vest stopped in his tracks and started pulling his vest over his head.

"I said pull it up, numbnuts, not get undressed."

Sweater Vest stopped, his sweater pulled clear of his head, but his arms still in the armholes. "I thought this would look more natural, like I was too warm ..."

Guy reached over and pulled the geek's button-down dress shirt out of his waistband, jerking it up to nipple height, then slid his hand to either side, pushing the confused geek to turn, so he could slide his hand across the back, across the shoulder blades, then down to the waistband of his usual Dockers. The geek had the physique of a corpse three days in the river, all soft and bloated, but no wires.

"Nobody's watching," said Guy as he flipped his companion's shirt back down, "so I don't care how it looks. Just bein' careful. You being so direct, it made me think you might be wired for sound is all. Had to check, you know, to be sure. Paranoia, it's part of the business ... tradecraft and all that shit. You need to learn that if you're going to be helping out."

Sweater Vest looked up from tucking in his shirt. "So, I guess that means you've decided I'm helping out."

Guy started walking again. "It means the hypothetical guy I know is interested in seeing whether you can be of use. Understand? He is commissioning a piece of *fiction* from you—a plot summary of sorts. He is interested in learning more about writers and wants to see how you would plot a situational inconveniencing in one of your mystery books." He looked over at Sweater Vest, who had again skipped a step to get in sync as Guy strolled along. "You do write mysteries, right? I'm ... He's dealing with a professional here, like himself."

Sweater Vest swallowed. "I just finished up a mystery recently."

"Good."

Sweater Vest nodded once, then pursed his lips, as if calculating something. "So, let's start out with the basics. Name and address ..."

Guy stopped him with a soccer-mom-in-a-fender-bender arm swing. "No names ... no addresses."

Sweater Vest practically screeched to a halt, his mouth gaping open. "I didn't mean yours ... I understand the confidential nature of the relationship. I meant, you know, the ... uh ... potential target ... of inconveniencing."

Guy turned to face his co-conspirator head-on. "I ain't gonna tell you that, neither. Not on your virgin run."

"But, but," Sweater Vest whined, throwing up his hands, "but how am I supposed to plot a scenario without details about the target? I need to research potential methods, plausible motives, possible patsies. I can't write blind. I need a prompt of some sort."

"Next time, sure. I understand your need for context. But you gotta understand my needs, too." He curled up his beefy hands into fists for a moment and then relaxed just enough to point one figure, gesticulating with quick jabs as he explained the situation. "I give you a name and I don't know what you're gonna do. You could run to the cops. You might give the target a heads up. That puts me at risk. That might let the target get away, go into hiding or some shit. Then I can't do the job and I disappoint my client. Hell, it might even expose my client to danger, if you warn the target and the target knows who might be looking to whack him."

"I ... I ... won't do th-that," Sweater Vest stammered.

"You say that now, kiddo, but I don't know what kind of backbone you got under that flabby exterior. Maybe you think you're tough, that you got the *cajonés* for this shit, but then you get home and you start second-guessing and getting all *Lifetime* movie, bawling your eyes out over some sentimental nonsense about morality and crap, and all of a sudden I'm up shit creek." He paused for a moment, uncurling his fists and sticking his hands into his pockets. "I need to make sure you're invested. Understand? We need a test run, where you don't have so much to go on that I'm at risk, but which shows you got something to offer and ends up with you having some skin in the game. *Capiche?*"

"Er ... yeah ... I mean yes. I understand."

Guy gave him a curt nod. "So, here's how it's gonna work. I give you some generic information about the job, but nothing that identifies or implicates anyone. You do your writer stuff and give me a plot outline ..." He cut off Sweater Vest before he could interrupt. "Yeah, yeah. I know it won't be your best work, being you don't have details on relatives, occupation, blah, blah, blah. But that's okay. We rendezvous next week, say outside that crap Mexican place where we first connected. Same day and time as this go around. You chat me up and give me what you got. I take care of business. If you read the papers, you'll see the fruits of your labors. You hold it together and then next time, you can get more creative because by then, y'see, you'll have something to lose if you get cold feet and turn rat. Understood?"

Sweater Vest licked his lips. "A bit of a mixed metaphor there at the end ..."

"Understood?" Guy barked.

"Understood."

"Good. So here's what we got ..."

#

Harold stared at the notes he'd hastily scribbled onto index cards after he had gotten back to the car following his meeting with Guy, then glanced back at the blank screen on his desktop. Finally, he typed "Plot Ideas" in boldface, centered on the page. Then, he sat, looking at the page, for almost twenty minutes without typing anything.

What was happening? He'd never had writer's block before. He didn't believe in writer's block. Writer's block was what amateurs and newbies and wannabe-writers got, not what pros like himself got. Why, he hadn't hesitated for more than a moment when he wrote his last letter to the editor. And the cat mystery had flowed forth onto the screen of his computer like fake movie blood in a slasher flick. He'd hardly made any revisions at all before he sent it in.

Could it be that he had qualms about the nature of his writing assignment? That he was worried about the fact someone was going to *die* in the manner he described?

That was stupid. Guy was a professional hit man. This target was doomed, with or without his literary flourishes. And Guy never got caught, so it wasn't as if he was enabling a murder—aiding and abetting or some such legal nonsense. He was merely making the job more ... entertaining. Even the I.R.S. classified writers as entertainers. With his writerly assistance, the death would be more interesting and less mundane.

If you really thought about it, the cops should thank him for his service. After all, investigating professional hits was, no doubt, boring and frustrating. The cops saw the same tired m.o. every time there was a professional hit and knew from the start they had no hope of catching the killer. This way, they'd have some variety and some hope of solving the crime, even if it was false hope.

The victim's family should probably thank him, too. With his literary flourishes, the murder would be more likely to generate more press than a garden-variety hit. That would make them think their loved one's demise was a more important event, which, in turn, would make them think their loved one was more important and, thus, their grief more justified. The attention their grief generated would make them think they were, themselves, more important, more newsworthy, more deserving of sympathy—boosting their self-esteem and enabling them to deal better with their own loss.

So, his words would have a profound, positive impact on the world. Plus, he was getting paid. Wasn't that what every writer yearned for?

He looked up at the screen.

This time, words were filling the page as his fingers poked and prodded the keyboard into submission. He had to admit it, this idea was really killer, in every sense of the word.

#

By the time he was done, it was well past midnight and he was bleary-eyed. He could compensate by sleeping in the next morning, except he never missed a meeting of the PMWGCS. True, he didn't have anything new to submit to the group ... and he was too tired to write anything else now ... but the group depended on him. After all, he'd already reviewed and critiqued this week's submissions. That effort ... those comments ... would be wasted if he didn't show up to tell the group's members what was wrong with their writing. They needed his insight, his example, and his presence to function.

He couldn't disappoint his fans.

#

Two hours into the PMWGCS meeting, Harold wished he had slept in, instead. Gantry was a no-show due to his current book tour. Minx was sullen. The latest quatrains in Bryce's epic poem were marred by a series of near rhymes. Civil War or no, the man shouldn't use the word "Gettysburg" if he couldn't find a decent multi-syllabic rhyme to go with it. Myrtle and Felicity got into an extended discussion about the types of flowers preferred by dragonflies. Steely Slash Rab announced he was leaving early to attend a sit-in at the town's new butcher shop, protesting that it shouldn't be located so close to an elementary school because it encouraged kids to become carnivores. And Carl droned on for nearly ten minutes about rehab for his hip replacement. Didn't he understand that the whole purpose of the PMWGCS was writing, not people? Carl should socialize with the other stiffs-in-waiting at the retirement home, not waste the group's time by talking about *life* instead of talking about *writing*.

By the time the group broke up for the morning, Harold wanted nothing more than to bolt for the door.

Unfortunately, Bryce blocked his path. "Hack, dude! You didn't turn in anything this week. Did you take my advice and give up writing entirely?"

Harold felt his lip curl into a scowl. "I'm working on something ... a mystery, if you must know."

"Mice? Gerbils? Or have you graduated to the big time of dog mysteries? I can see it now, *The Butt Snifferer*. He tracks down criminals by day and drinks out of the toilet by night. I'm sure you could find a market for that."

"Actually, I've got a buyer already. I'm submitting my piece on Tuesday, so there won't be time for the group to critique it." Harold regretted the words as soon as he said them, but there was no going back. He just prayed Bryce wouldn't ask the publisher's name or to see a copy of his mystery in print.

Fortunately, Bryce seemed to think he already had all the answers. "Let me guess. *Self-Publish America*, right? You do know their reputation, don't you? It's a vanity press scheme, Hack. Those guys will publish anything ... *anything*."

"I don't think so," Harold replied.

"Why's that?"

"I couldn't find any epic poetry in their catalog."

"Fuck you, Hack. Fuck you."

Chapter 8

Sweater Vest showed up as instructed, grasping a small sheaf of papers. Guy said nothing. He simply held out a hand. Sweater Vest gave him three or four pages, but kept the other half for himself.

"Whadya do? Make a copy for the cops?" growled Guy.

His cohort jumped at the word "cops."

"No! No, nothing like that. I just have a copy for myself, so we can each look at our own copy as we ... as you review the work and we chat about any questions or clarifications. That way I'm not looking over your shoulder all the time."

Guy wrinkled up his nose. "That's good, cuz I spend enough time looking over my own shoulder. Don't need you to be doing that, too."

Sweater Vest forced a nervous chuckle that sounded more like the traditional turn-your-head-and-cough than actual amusement.

"Jesus," continued Guy, "don't just stand there and watch me read."

"Uh ... okay." The scribe looked around, then shuffled toward the storefront of a nearby pawn shop.

A casual observer would think Sweater Vest (who was actually wearing a simple dress shirt and sports coat atop jeans today) was perusing items in the window, but Guy could tell the writer was actually still watching him read, only by reflection now. Guy grunted and turned his back to his potential partner in crime.

He finished the pages, then flipped back to scan the high points a second time. Finally, he turned back toward his friend, who had given up any pretense of not watching him, and blurted out: "I don't get it."

"What do you mean you don't get it? What part don't you get?"

Guy sighed as Sweater Vest scurried over. "The car part. Why am I breaking into the garage and starting the target's car?"

"To make the death look like a suicide or maybe accidental." Sweater Vest held up his own copy and pointed at an early sentence. "See, here, you go to the house on a stormy, rainy night ..."

"Okay, so it's a dark and stormy night. Why?"

"It covers up the noise and washes away any evidence on the driveway."

Guy kinked one leg up to show his shoes. "Size eleven. Common brand. I ditch them afterwards, along with my clothes. Not too worried about it."

Sweater Vest pursed his lips, as if hesitating over contradicting Guy. "Dusty shoe prints on the driveway might not get you caught, but they are evidence of foul play. You have to change your mindset. You don't want the police to think this is a homicide at all."

Sweater Vest started to point again, but Guy cut him off. "Just talk me through it."

"Oh, okay. So, well, you go on a stormy night and you go into the garage, but you don't leave any signs of forced entry. No broken windows or doors. You just pick the lock if the side door isn't open."

"No worries there. I can finesse the lock without any clumsy, tell-tale signs."

"Good. So you let yourself in, but as you go in, you put on these plastic booties, you know, like they use at open houses at high-end mansions in the suburbs, so you don't track in any water and leave footprints inside the garage and you don't carry out with you any oil or other evidence you were in the garage."

"Jeez, kid. You watch too much *C.S.I.* on television. No suburban police department has the budget to analyze that crap."

"They're just plastic booties. You can get a hundred pairs for six bucks at an office supply store."

Guy shrugged. "Whatever."

"You look around and make sure the garage is sealed tight. No open windows, no outside vents, no gaps in the doorway. If you find any holes, you stuff 'em with steel wool ..."

"... cuz that won't be suspicious."

"No, it won't," snapped Sweater Vest. The fellow obviously didn't take criticism too well. "Steel wool is what people use to stop-up cracks and holes where mice can get in."

"Really?" said Guy. "Not much of a mice problem in the city. I guess the rats must eat 'em."

"Then you start up the car ..."

"So now I'm breaking into the car and hotwiring it?"

"It's the suburbs. Nobody locks their car in their own garage."

"So, just the hotwiring, then."

Sweater Vest huffed. "Only if the keys aren't in the ignition or in the visor and there's no magnetic hide-a-key in the wheel well."

"Fine," Guy huffed back. "Let's assume I can start the car. Won't the target hear that?"

"Not on a stormy night!"

Guy rolled his eyes. "Then what?"

"You start the car, leave it idling, and sneak out the door, removing your booties as you leave."

"And then?"

"And then, what?" replied Sweater Vest.

"And then how do I gank the guy?" barked Guy. "Strangulation?" His fingers twitched to rehearse the scene with Sweater Vest as the target.

"You don't have to gank the guy. You're done. The guy dies on his own time. The next morning he gets up and steps into his garage to head for work or whatever. He gets in and notices the keys in the ignition, but the car won't start because it ran out of gas sometime during the night, after idling for several hours. Then the built-up carbon monoxide in the car and the garage kills him while you're having whiskey and cornflakes for breakfast or are sleeping in. Best of all, people think it was a suicide."

Guy thought for a minute. "Yeah, I can see how that might go, but it's not the only possibility. You gotta be ready for contingencies."

Sweater Vest glared at him. "Like what?"

Guy screwed up his nose and thought for a second. "What if he passes out before he gets in the car? You know, from the carbon monoxide."

Sweater Vest gave Guy a hand-shrug, palms up. "So what? Maybe they still think it's suicide. Maybe the local detectives, they think he accidentally left the car running in a closed garage. Still doesn't spell murder."

"Speaking about detecting, what if the fellow, he has those carbon monoxide detector thingies?"

"You look for 'em and take out the batteries. People leave detectors around without batteries all the time. They can't stand it when they beep to indicate the battery's low. Especially 'cause the beeping just wears out the battery faster."

"Okay," said Guy, "but what about the big garage door? Won't the carbon monoxide be dissipated as soon as he pushes the button on the automatic garage door opener when he first comes out of the house?"

Sweater Vest scowled. "If he's got an automatic opener, just disable it. You could short it out or just trip the GFI interrupter for the outlet, or the circuit breaker for the whole damn garage." Sweater Vest's hands began to grasp and ungrasp, as if he now wanted to strangle something ... someone. "If you don't like that idea, you can pull a bolt on the assemblage that connects the door to the track, then leave the bolt and nut scattered on the floor, so it looks like they just popped because the bolt was loose and vibrated off." Sweater Vest's tone was cool and growing colder. "Or you could simply pull the handle that disconnects the door from the opener so it can still be opened in case the power goes off in a storm. The first two approaches could be viewed as consistent with an accidental death; the last one is consistent with suicide. That's what I'd do if I was offing myself and wanted to make sure I couldn't easily save myself at the last minute just by thumbing the opener in the car."

Jesus. Who thinks about such stuff?

But Guy didn't let that thought throw him off subject. He had a one-track mind when it came to work. "But, what if he's got an electric car ... or a hybrid that shuts itself off when it idles? What if the carbon monoxide concentration isn't high enough or he smells the fumes and goes back inside? What if he hears the car or I don't disable the alarm or he comes in the garage when I'm there?"

Sweater Vest simply stared at him for a few moments, his brow furrowed, his eyes flicking, his teeth clenched, his face quivering. Finally he spoke in a low, ice-cold monotone. "Then you pull out your .22 and put one in the back of his head, *like you always do*. You won't be any worse off for having tried to make it look like a suicide, now will you?"

The kid was right. You want to change something in your life, you gotta change something in your life. "Fine," he said. "Watch the news. If this works the way you say, you meet me at the park again, the Tuesday following. Same time."

Sweater Vest gave him a single nod, a small smile snarking across his tight lips, but then the smile faltered. "How do I know when you do it, so I can check the papers in the days following?"

Guy chuckled. "Simple. It'll be a dark and stormy night."

Chapter 9

Harold swore as he picked up his newspaper from the driveway. Though bagged, it was a heavy, soggy mess, just like yesterday's. Damn delivery guy. No one had any respect for the written word anymore. It had taken him more than two hours to dry yesterday's paper, peeling the pages back one by one to check the police blotter and local news sections. All for nothing.

He slit off the plastic with a utility knife and laid the paper on his kitchen counter, where he had a high-intensity desk lamp still set up from the day before. He switched on the bulb and attended to his morning routine, pouring himself a jumbo tumbler of RC Cola and grabbing a hunk of frosted cinnamon Danish while the lamp seared the paper dry.

He forced himself to spend time reviewing and critiquing submissions for next week's PMWGCS session in the meantime. It had to get done sooner or later and this was the perfect time to do it. He often commented on other people's alleged writing when he was in a bad mood. It helped keep him from self-censoring his remarks—being nice wouldn't do the conglomeration of amateur scribes who made up the group any favors. By the time he had savaged Steely Slash Rab's rap lyrics, close-edited Carl's vivid remembrances of tactical maneuvers between the sheets into more lurid and less military prose, cut eight paragraphs of Moby-Dickish exposition about the wonders of dragonfly anatomy out of Myrtle's endless fantasy quest, pointed out beat-count consistency issues in Bryce's epic re-telling of the first salvos of the Civil War, declared Felicity's latest nature poems unpublishable, and fantasized about Minx before writing "Nice Effort!!!" on the last page of her meandering mumbling about death, sex, and body piercings, the newspaper was finally dry enough for inspection.

He found what he was looking for on page ten of the Local section, across from the beginning of the obituaries on page eleven:

Police Investigating Death of Plant Manager as Possible Suicide: *The body of local resident Robert Dobolina was discovered Thursday afternoon in the garage of his home at 362 Sycamore Street. Officials at Bodursky Plastic Containers became concerned at Mr. Dobolina's unexplained absence for a second day and, after failing to reach him at home or by cell telephone, contacted his wife, who was visiting with out-of-state relatives. She, in turn, asked a neighbor to check the house.*

The neighbor, Grace Masterson, located Mr. Dobolina slumped over the steering wheel of his vehicle in the closed garage of the Dobolina residence. According to police sources, Mrs. Masterson immediately dialed 9-1-1 to report an apparent heart attack and began administering CPR. Upon arrival, first responders pronounced Mr. Dobolina dead. Subsequent investigation revealed Mr. Dobolina had passed away sometime on Wednesday morning, apparently of carbon monoxide poisoning.

Confidential sources indicate the vehicle's ignition was turned on, but that the car had run out of gas. The Coroner has listed the death as a possible suicide.

Mr. Dobolina is survived by his wife, Connie, and by his sons Avery and Robert, Jr. Service details are pending.

Harold flushed with excitement as he read the words, savoring the details. Maybe it was the lingering aftermath of his Minx fantasy, but he stirred with almost orgasmic delight as he read the words "possible suicide." That was him; that was his plot. He had done that. He had led the neighbor, the first responders, the coroner, the police, even the news to the fictional place he had wanted them to go. He had created his own little universe where his fiction held sway, where his words were the law. Like the real universe, his would expand. The wife and the kids, they might have doubts now, but Dobolina's "suicide" would become a foundational pillar of their future existence. The police would box up his story, shelve it in the evidence locker, and declare it closed. The insurance company would deny payment under the suicide exclusion—they should be giving him a cut of their savings, if you really thought about it—and the Church would deny the deceased burial in sanctified ground. Maybe the Devil, himself, would claim Dobolina's soul. After all, suicide is a mortal sin and he, Harold J. Ackerman, writer extraordinaire, had created a suicide out of paper, pen, and imagination.

And to top it all off, he was being paid by an undoubtedly now very satisfied client. Even better than getting paid to write was getting paid to write a sequel. Once you made that first sale, the next one was easier and the next easier yet as the series continued into infinity.

He cut the article out of the newspaper, trimming the edges carefully so they were straight and true, then tucked the clipping into the corner of the screen on his desktop, where it could inspire him for generations ... for universes ... to come.

#

Grinning broadly, Sweater Vest raised his hand high into the air as he approached Guy, like he wanted to fucking high-five.

Guy kept his hands in his pockets. "Dial down the enthusiasm, dipshit," he growled. "We're professionals. I'm a professional. Act like a fucking professional."

Sweater Vest flinched, almost as if he had been slapped—not a fighting slap, but the kind of backhanded slap with a glove that people were always giving in period movies when they wanted to duel or some gentlemanly shit like that. Finally, he recovered and spoke. "I was ... I was just celebrating our success. Everything worked out just like I said it would, didn't it?"

Guy wriggled his nose. Jeez, he hated working with a partner. There was a reason he liked working solo, he remembered. No need to stroke the ego of a partner or worry about what they might do or say ... or want. "Yeah, kid. Right. Everything worked out like you said."

"The cops are clueless. They've got no idea this was a professional hit. They aren't even looking for us. We did a great job!"

"We? I did my usual, competent, low-key work. Us? They wouldn't ever be looking for us, kiddo. They'd be looking for me, not you. The only way they'd ever be looking for you is if you shoot your mouth off ... or if they get to me, which they won't do unless you can't keep your trap shut." He sighed. "You did fine, kid, but part of the gig is keepin' a low profile and never talking about what you've done." He motioned with his head for Sweater Vest to follow and began to lumber down the street toward the park. "So let's not talk about the past and instead focus on the future. I've got a new assignment for you. Bit trickier than the last. The good news is that you've got more time to work up a ... scenario."

#

Harold rubbed at his chin. Suicide just wouldn't work this time. Nobody would buy it. The target was well off, well-liked, outgoing, and chipper in all of the usual annoying ways that happy people inflicted upon the rest of the world. Harold couldn't depend on making it look like an accident. Not only were accidents tough to pull off, he ran the risk that if the police looked too hard at an accident, they would discover it wasn't accidental. That would spur them to look for a murderer and that could lead to Guy.

No, much better to make this one a clear murder and hand the police a patsy on a platter. Cops were lazy. Give them a suspect and a handful of circumstantial evidence and they were happy to pass on the case to the District Attorney and chalk up a collar to pad their statistics before their next performance review.

He surfed around the Facebook pages of the target's friends and family for a bit. The sister was a possibility. Her posts had that desperate quality of a pathetic loser, always complaining about her life, her health, her crappy car, and her long-distance, sports-obsessed boyfriend. Maybe he could sell jealousy as a motive or, if he was lucky and she got something under her dead brother's last will and testament, financial gain.

He checked her FB and Twitter timelines for posting patterns. She never posted during her favorite television shows—angsty dramas featuring pretty young people facing vampires, stale fantasy tropes, and other adversities between bouts of bedding one another. In other words, a fan of Thursday night on The CW. As a dedicated enthusiast with limited income, she undoubtedly would be DVRing the shows so she could watch again without paying for a download or waiting for the DVD/BlueRay. So, no real proof she was watching TV live, like anyone but losers did that anymore. That meant he could tell Guy to time the murder during her favorite shows and she would have no alibi and an electronic trail that could be explained away by the cops.

He had a plan. He had a start. And that was all a real writer needs.

If he worked hard, he could have an outline done before *America's Got Talent* started. If only they had a reality show for writers, he could be a contestant. He could be a star.

#

"But I always use five stars at the left margin to designate a scene break," mumbled Myrtle at the next session of the PMWGCS. "I've done that for every scene break in the last twelve hundred pages of my novel."

Felicity frowned and rapped the table with her pen. "The author's not allowed to speak during a critique," she admonished. "You know better, Myrtle."

Harold bristled at the interruption. "Which means I've marked the change at least three hundred times on the hard copies of comments I've turned back in to you, all to no effect, whatsoever. And, they're asterisks, not 'stars.'"

Myrtle stared fiercely at Harold and clenched her mouth shut.

Harold continued. "As I was saying, the correct way to designate a scene break within a chapter, whether to indicate a passage of time or a change of point-of-view character, is a new line with a single, centered octothorpe."

"Excuse me?" exclaimed Felicity.

"No," growled Bryce, with a glance over at Felicity. "Excuse me." He turned toward Harold. "What the fucking hell is an octothorpe?"

"Oh, my," murmured Myrtle.

"Can you use it in a sentence?" queried Steely Slash Rab.

Harold smiled. All eyes were on him, seeking his expertise. This was how the PMWGCS should be. "The designation of an octothorpe typically appears above the numeral '3' on a computer keyboard."

Bryce screwed up his face for a moment as almost everyone else scrambled to extract their laptops from briefcase or purse.

Bryce beat them to the punch. "You mean a 'pound' sign? A 'hash' mark?"

Harold sniffed. "That's what the common masses generally call it, but the word 'octothorpe' is much more precise and descriptive. 'Octo,' of course, means 'eight,' designating the eight points of the symbology. The symbol was once used by typesetters to indicate a place where space should be added and became a convenient symbol for use by phone and computer companies to indicate something special was about to appear in dialing or coding instructions."

Bryce's face was reddening, an indication of apoplectic elevation of blood pressure, no doubt. "Are you fucking kidding me?" he asked. "Wait, let me tweet this to all my friends and followers." He plucked a Galaxy smartphone from his front shirt pocket and began typing furiously with his thumbs as he spoke the works aloud. "This ... guy ... in my ... writers' ... group ... is ... a ... pompous ... asshole. Octothorpe ... surroundedbyidiots ... HASHTAG ... surroundedbyidiots."

"Oh, my ..." whispered Felicity.

"Oh, dear ..." muttered Myrtle.

"Damn cellphones!" growled Sergeant Pilkington.

"Will you follow me on Twitter?" pleaded Steely Slash Rab, looking toward Bryce.

Gantry Ellis cleared his throat and everyone fell silent.

"Gotta admit," the bestselling author drawled. "Harold is right about the use of the term in the computer and telephony industries. Ran into it when I was researching NSA spying techniques with some Sprint employees."

Harold sat up straight and jutted out his jaw. "See, Gantry agrees with me."

Gantry made a gentle downward motion with his hands palms down, as if indicating Harold should slow down. "Being technically correct isn't the point. A lot of industry jargon, of course, is of ... er ... limited utility in the workaday world."

Harold glared at him.

Felicity took charge once again. "Anything you want to say in response to the group's comments, Myrtle?"

Myrtle pursed her lips a moment before speaking. "Thank you, as always, for your comments. As to the scene breaks, well ... I guess I'll let the copyeditor deal with such things after I've sold my epic. I mean, isn't that what editors are for?"

No verbal octothorpe here. Felicity barely waited for Myrtle to finish talking before she spoke up again. "That brings us to Harold's submission, a chapter from a murder mystery novel. Who'd like to go first?"

Bryce spoke up. "Well, he's real consistent about his use of octothorpes, though the use of the automatic first line indentation feature means they're actually to the right of center when he simply centers the line without backspacing to eliminate the indentation first ..."

Felicity's brow furrowed as she gave Bryce a squint-eyed look. "Any *substantive comments* on the submission?"

Minx signaled for attention by wriggling her fingers, her shiny black nail polish flashing under the bright lights of the Township office. "I think the bit about doing the murder during the time slots she was DVRing her favorite TV shows was kind of a clever way to undercut her alibi. I mean, I wouldn't think of that if I was planning a murder and trying to frame someone else for it. Who sits around their apartment just thinking about stuff like how to get away with killing people by framing other people? It's impressive ... in kind of an excitingly creepy way ... but impressive. Kind of like a sexy horror movie." Minx looked directly at Harold and batted her long, black eyelashes. "Harold's definitely showing us a new view of himself."

Harold, of course, couldn't respond during the critique of his submission, but his stirring loins didn't know that. He closed his eyes for a moment and visualized really showing Minx a new view of himself as she looked up at him, her long-lashed eyelids half closed in pleasure.

Steely Slash Rab broke the mood by clearing his throat. "I agree with Minx, but I'm also a bit confused about the larger context of this submission. It's not exactly a who-dunnit, what with us knowing that the real killer is setting up the sister as the killer. And, it's not exactly a crime procedural, since we know the killer's whole plan. I guess it's more of a mystery as to whether and how the real killer's going to get caught, but I'm not sure. Going straight to—what is it, chapter nine?— without reading the other chapters first, makes it a bit hard to comment on. Still, even though I liked some of the technical bits, I was a bit underwhelmed by the sister's supposed motivation for killing her brother. Without a compelling motive, the frame's incomplete and unsatisfying. I mean, I get that she's depressed and maybe jealous 'cause she's not as rich and successful as he is, but that's been true for decades. Why would she kill him now? What's the last straw that supposedly pushes her over the edge into crime?"

"Women can be moody," growled Carl with steely authority. "Never can tell what might set them off. Could be that it was her time ..."

"You just stop right there, Sergeant!" barked out Felicity, giving Carl a stern stare.

Carl held up his hands and shot a look of wide-eyed innocence back at her. "What'd I do? I was just saying that maybe her time in therapy had brought some issues to the surface that she'd repressed earlier."

"That, that repression thing," interrupted Bryce, "is a good idea, but I don't think repressed jealousy is a big enough motivator for murder for the frame to stick. What if the real killer planted some evidence of a traumatic event from the sister's childhood, something she could blame on her brother? Maybe he broke her toys or locked her in a closet or something."

Gantry chimed in. "I like where you're going, Bryce, but you need to go bigger, more traumatic. Something darker, more perverted, as a motive." He cocked his head to one side for a moment. "Incest is always good."

Bryce smirked. "Can I quote you on that?"

Gantry fluttered a hand in Bryce's direction in dismissal. "You know what I mean. Leaving some suggestion of some sexual event between the two, consensual or non-consensual, years in the past would give the cops plenty of motive."

"But, I don't understand," cooed Myrtle. "Nothing like that ever happened, right? The murderer is just making it up to frame someone else. Won't the sister just deny it when the police ask her about it?"

"That's the thing," replied Gantry. "Sure, she'll deny it. But, that's what she would do if she was the real murderer. And, given the delicate nature of the subject matter, the cops will approach it obliquely, with broad, open-ended questions. You know, something like 'Did your brother ever do anything bad when you were younger?' or 'Did anything bad ever happen to you?'" Gantry shrugged his shoulders. "Remember, they're looking to confirm a motive. Once they have an answer that confirms their suspicions, they'll stop asking questions."

"But that's not why the sister is in therapy," protested Myrtle.

Bryce jumped back into the discussion. "But, the therapist is bound by patient confidentiality. She can't say squat."

"That's not true," interjected Steely Slash Rab. "She could waive privilege."

Bryce shook his head. "She does that and the police can ask the therapist anything, like whether she hated her brother or ever expressed any dark or violent thoughts. Everybody tells their therapist something they don't want to get out. Fear of embarrassment is a powerful thing."

"That's all true," Gantry said, "but you're missing the most important point. Don't you see? Incest is absolutely perfect."

"Oh," replied Bryce. "We've moved from 'always good' to 'absolutely perfect.' Are you sure I can't quote you on that?"

Gantry sighed. "Sentences, like words, only have true meaning in *situ*. A suggestion of incest as the motivation here is more powerful in assisting an effort to frame the sister for at least four reasons. One, as we've already discussed, is that incest is such a strong taboo that the subsequent denials by the sister, even if they were not made in the context of denying a murder charge, are easily explainable and understood by a jury. Two, there is almost no way to prove that the incest did or did not occur, especially so many years ago. Three, incest is an especially powerful motivation for murder. And, four, the precipitating event for the murder is so heinous, itself, that the police and the prosecutors are more likely to go easy on the defendant and try to avoid a trial."

Harold took notes feverishly, attempting to get Gantry's exact phrasing.

I don't understand," said Felicity. "Why would the authorities want to avoid trial if the case is so strong because the motivation is so powerful?"

Gantry sat back, as if used to lecturing on such topics. "If the victim is really a pillar of the community, the police won't ... and the victim's family won't ... want to tarnish the guy's reputation unnecessarily. To the extent they believe the motive, they'll also feel sorry for the sister. Not so much that they'll encourage vigilante justice by letting her go, but enough so they'll be amenable to plea bargaining to a lesser charge, say manslaughter. That's the key to a perfect frame up. The lower the charge they are willing to offer the suspect, the less punishment the suspect faces. If the plea is a really sweet deal as compared to what the suspect risks after an expensive, embarrassing, and debilitating trial, the more likely the suspect—*even an innocent suspect*—will take the deal. And once the cops have a conviction, even on a plea, there is almost no chance they will entertain, much less be looking for, someone else as the perpetrator. Once the sister takes a plea, the frame is perfect."

Yes. That's all Harold wanted. The perfect frame. He couldn't be happier.

Of course, Bryce had to stomp on his moment.

"That takes care of motivation, but I still think the frame needs a bit more work on the circumstantial evidence side. I mean, won't the cops be asking questions about whether anyone saw the sister or the sister's car in the neighborhood?"

Myrtle rejoined the conversation. "Don't forget cameras. There's a spy camera on every corner. They're everywhere, watching everybody every single moment these days. It's not right."

Carl nodded. "The crime lab guys, they can sync 'em all up and see who drove where when. That's what they did for that bastard, McVeigh, down in Oklahoma City. Synced up every video camera in town and tracked him driving that Ryder van in front of that federal building he blew up. You know, the one with the daycare center on the first floor."

Gantry leaned forward. "Most police departments, they don't have the budget for the kind of thing you see on those crime procedural shows. They're overworked and overwhelmed. They can't test DNA in a few minutes and send agents all over town looking for random videos to review. Just doesn't happen, even for a murder. Especially in a small town. Big case like, say, the JonBenet thing, that can bankrupt a police department, maybe even a whole town." He looked over at Bryce. "Not saying that the circumstantial evidence couldn't use a bit of a boost—just no reason to get too complicated about it. Simple is good."

Simple was good. Guy seemed like a simple guy to Harold and Harold already had a few simple ideas on how to plant a few extra bits of evidence to go along with the boosted evidence of motive the PMWGCS had helped him polish up.

If only they knew how clever he really was.

Chapter 10

"So, why exactly am I boosting the sister's car to do the deed? I don't like depending on an unknown vehicle for my getaway. You know what I mean?" Guy kept on reading as Sweater Vest considered his answer. The plan for this hit was considerably more complicated than the last one and even that one had been more complicated than his usual routine. "And what if she notices it's missing while I'm out on the job? Getting boosted for grand theft auto is bad enough, but when you're still carrying a murder weapon, it's downright stupid."

Sweater Vest frowned and gave him the kind of deep sigh that Sister Agnes had always given Guy when returning his exam papers back at St. Joseph's Academy. "She won't report the car stolen. She'll be engrossed in her favorite TV programs. They run back-to-back for two hours every Thursday night." Sweater Vest paused for a moment as he flipped through his papers. "And, as I noted on page six, she drives a Hyundai. They've got the best warranty on the market, so I doubt she is haphazard about getting needed repairs done." He looked up. "Just remember to wear gloves ..."

"Duh."

"... and adjust the seat back to its original position when you return the car. You're taller than her and you don't want her or, heaven forbid, the police to notice the seat is set for someone else. And, while we're at it, don't fuss with the mirrors at all. You can drive without well-aimed mirrors for the short distance you have to travel."

Guy suppressed a growl. He wasn't an idiot. And, even if he was, he didn't need some snot-nosed suburban wordsmith treating him like he was. He'd done plenty of jobs before he met this jerk. Plenty.

Still, he had to admit that the plan was pretty solid. That bit about manufacturing evidence of an accusation of incest was spot on. The cops, once they found something like that, they'd never let go. They'd be all over dear old sis, for sure, which meant they wouldn't be looking for him. And if sis copped a plea, the case would be closed.

Sure, he'd never been caught on any of his hits, but as far as he knew they were all still open cases. Cold, yeah, but still open. Once they pinned this job on the sister, they'd never nail him for it. They'd be too embarrassed to even try and, if they weren't, he'd still have the sister's confession and conviction for reasonable doubt.

That's what you do when you plead out, you have to confess. And he always did his best to avoid confessing to anything. Learned that at St. Joseph's Academy, too.

Boosting the car still nagged at him. It wasn't that he didn't know how, but his first instinct was to avoid added risk.

"But how can we be sure anyone will ever know the car was there? It's not like I wanna attract attention. It seems like I'm complicating things for no sure payoff."

Sweater Vest pondered a moment. "Just drive up over the curb a bit onto the grass when you're leaving. It'll leave a tire impression that can be traced, even if no one notices the car parked at her brother's place while you're inside."

Did cops even do that Plaster of Paris crap anymore?

"Ooohh," said Sweater Vest, "even better. Scrape the side of the car against the curbside mailbox as you leave. They'll be able to match up the scratch and the paint trace conclusively.

Yeah. That could work.

"Alright. I'm onboard there. But, poison? Seems a bit frou-frou for my taste. Gun's quicker."

"Women tend to use poison. They don't have the physical strength for knives and we don't want to have to worry about blood spatter and GSR and how and where she got the gun. Cyanide's quick. Got the formula online and printed it out for you. Ingredients are easy to get. Just slip some in whatever he's drinking and wait for him to down the stuff. It will be over fast."

"How can you be so sure?" Guy responded. "You done this yourself?"

"Of course not," sniffed Sweater Vest, as if he was somehow better than Guy. "I know from the Tylenol poisonings. At one point they were getting so many calls from people worried they'd been poisoned by cyanide from the Tylenol they took that they put a recording on their hotline number that said 'If you took Tylenol and are worried you ingested cyanide, you haven't. Because if you had, you'd already be dead.'"

"Is that true?" Guy was shocked. Even he knew that would be lousy PR for a company, to be so blunt.

Sweater Vest shrugged and fluttered his left hand. "Who knows? I read it on the internet."

"Well, it kinda matters whether it's true to me," gruffed Guy.

"The tale is consistent with my research into the time co-efficient for concentrated cyanide poisoning. That's why spies and astronauts use them."

"Astronauts?"

Sweater Vest looked at him like he had suggested strangling a puppy. "Well, you don't expect them to just wait to suffocate if they get stranded up there, do you?"

Wow. This guy spent way too much time reading stuff on the internet.

"You want me to slip the cyanide into the guy's Tang, too?"

"What?"

"Never mind," Guy groused. "Cyanide it is."

"If you spill a little cyanide on the car seat when you're done, you might get lucky and the sister will use the car before the police exam it ... or her ... and get some on her clothing. That would clinch things for sure."

"Okay, but let's not go overboard. I'm getting paid to off the guy, not frame the sister. I only care that the cops consider her the prime suspect. I don't have to make the case a slam-dunk."

Sweater Vest sniffed. "I'm a professional creator of alternative realities ... I build a complete world or I don't build one at all."

Guy swallowed hard. He got the impression Sweater Vest spent most of his time in fictional realities. Still, he said nothing. It didn't pay to irritate a co-conspirator. That was a fact in the real world, and that's where Guy lived and did business ... deadly business.

#

This death, a murder after all, made the front page of the Local section of the paper, below the fold. Harold read the article over RC Cola and Pop Tarts, then toasted up an extra Pop Tart and re-read it again. The piece, written in the bland authoritative style common to crime beat reporters, was pretty thin on details. No doubt the police were withholding information key to their pursuit of an active investigation. But the paper did say funeral arrangements were unavailable pending release of the body by a forensic pathologist in the Coroner's Office.

Harold made a mental note to watch the obituary notices for the next few days, until the service details were announced. After all, these people were *experiencing* something he wrote. He wanted to see the reviews.

#

"You did what?" Guy yelled, without thinking. He dialed down his continuing remarks to a barely restrained, low, rolling thunder. "Are you a fucking moron?" When Sweater Vest didn't immediately respond, he continued on. "You never, *never ever in a million years*, go to the funeral of a target. You understand?"

If he'd had a .22 in his hand, he might have offed Sweater Vest on the spot. Maybe even if he'd had a knife, like the one in that movie. It would be easy to gut the unsuspecting suburbanite *moron* on the spot, sit his body down on the park bench and move on with his day and his life, except he didn't have a knife on him at the moment. That was probably a good thing, because if he started stabbing this idiot, he wasn't sure he would be able to stop. Most crimes of passion probably had nothing to do with love or lust or sex, but they probably had plenty to do with someone being a fucking dipshit when someone else had a weapon in hand.

Sweater Vest's clueless, dumb stare finally resolved itself into a look of bewildered insult. " I ... I was just following through on the assignment."

Guy grabbed Sweater Vest's shoulder and leaned in to talk to him nose to nose, not caring if a little spittle sprayed forth as he punctuated each word for emphasis. "There ... is ... no ... follow-through ... on ... murder." Guy closed his eyes for a moment and shook his head in disbelief. "Once the hit is dead, you're through. Get it? Dead means done."

"Well, for you, sure." Sweater Vest rolled his eyes. He rolled his fucking eyes at Guy. "But for a writer to assess the effectiveness of his work, he has to see how the public reacts. He has to gauge whether they found the world he created not only credible, but compelling. In this instance, I wanted to see if the sister looked more frightened than sad, whether the target's family looked at the sister with accusation in their eyes, whether members of the community were less than whole-hearted in their expressions of sorrow, whether the police ..."

Guy actually felt his blood pressure skyrocket from its already elevated level. "Jesus, Mary, and Joseph! The police were there? What if they'd asked you why *you* were there?"

Sweater Vest made a face and scratched his cheek while he thought for a second, but Guy didn't have the patience for the wordsmith to work through his transitory writer's block. "Holy Mother of God, tell me they weren't taking pictures of the mourners. Tell me they weren't taking down the license plate numbers of all the cars at the cemetery.

Tell me you didn't do something so stupid that it's going to get you questioned or caught."

Sweater Vest wrinkled his brow, as if he were replaying the funeral scene in his head. "I don't remember seeing anyone with a camera ..."

Guy clenched and unclenched his fists. "See anyone with a *phone*, cuz that's all you need these days, a phone and a leisurely turn to take a panoramic shot of everyone everywhere. They can blow up the picture later and get all the details they need."

"Oh. I guess that's true. But, I don't recall anyone doing anything like that. I mean, not anything obvious."

"What if they figure out who you are and that you have no connection whatsoever to the deceased? What if they come to your door and want answers?"

"Well," Sweater Vest temporized, "I guess I'd just tell them ..."

Guy interrupted. "And don't say you'd just tell them you read about the murder in the paper and wanted to express your condolences. Nobody crashes graveside services. They crash weddings and wakes, cuz that's where the free booze is. Besides, I may not know you all that well, but even I can tell that you're not the kind of guy who has a reputation for spontaneous expressions of sympathy to random strangers. If this was a *Lifetime* movie, you'd get cast as the creepy dude who spends too much time watching kids at the park."

Guy could see Sweater Vest's blood pressure was rising, too. The fellow's face was flushing red and his jaw was clenched tight for a few moments before he responded. "There's no need to be insulting. I had ... I *have* ... a perfectly good reason to give should anyone ask me why I was at the funeral. It's the same reason I can give for being anywhere, anytime, watching anything from bums urinating on the subway platform to young women walking by in thin summer dresses. I'm a *writer*. My job is to observe things, notice them, experience them, memorize them, and keep them in my mind's eye for later use. Everything, everywhere is grist for my mill and I grind my flour into a soft, smooth, silky silt. Characters, settings, emotions, storylines, places, things, clothing, arcane bits of description and poetry. A writer has an excuse for knowing everything from nuclear weapon yields to whether college girls typically wear thongs to avoid panty-lines on their tight, tight jeans when they're attending a kegger at the local frat. I can go anywhere on the excuse of gathering atmosphere. I can ask questions about a building's security system or untraceable poisons or what knots are best used for S&M bondage sessions without blinking because I can always say it's research for a book. I don't even have to produce the book because I can always say I haven't written it yet."

Jesus, the kid was really wound tight.

"I'm a *writer*. I have the perfect excuse for anything. If I say something stupid or offensive or racist, I don't have to apologize, because I can say I said it to gauge reaction to make a scene or a bit of dialogue more realistic. If I want to take a needlepoint class, I don't have to be embarrassed, because I can say it's for a project I'm working on. If I want to loiter around a shop that sells sex toys or ask the local biker gang about their preferences in automatic weapons or purchase a battle axe, I can say it's for a book. Heck, I can even deduct it from my taxes. Look, people may not *like* writers. They may not respect them or pay them well. But they understand that writers are strange people who do strange things all the time. They tolerate them, like kids with Downs

Syndrome. They may not want to be around them and they may thank God they don't have one of them in the family, but they understand they can't help what they are and if you don't make eye contact or aggravate them too much, they'll wander off and be weird somewhere else real soon."

Sweater Vest paused for a moment before continuing, his voice calmer. "Listen, you don't need to worry about my end. I don't worry about yours. We're both professionals here. Just keep in mind that, should someone stumble across our friendship, I have a perfectly credible reason for talking to you. What's your reason for talking to me?"

Guy said nothing in response. If someone stumbled across his friendship with Sweater Vest, Sweater Vest soon wouldn't be talking to anyone at all but angels, but there was no percentage in saying that.

After a few moments, Sweater Vest's shoulders relaxed and the vein in his forehead stopped bulging. The passion and acrimony of his tirade was melting away. Finally, the kid wriggled his nose for a second and looked him in the eye, as if they were friends: "So, what've you got for me on our next assignment?"

Guy half-smiled at the kid. Things were back to business. "A two-fer. Middle-aged couple."

Sweater Vest tilted his head to one side. "Murder/Suicide?"

Guy shook his head. "Nah. No need for something that complicated. They live in a high crime area. I was thinking burglary gone bad, but you're the expert. Take a look at the details and get back to me in a couple weeks."

"That long?"

"I don't do more than a job a month, kid. Deaths spike too much and all of a sudden you got a task force or some shit to deal with—not that I think working by committee is a good way to solve crimes, but you can never tell when someone might have an actual good idea amidst all the crap and clutter flying about when people are talking and trying to impress each other."

Chapter 11

"Settle down, writers," cooed Felicity. "We can't all talk at once or all of our good ideas will be lost in the shuffle."

"Where's that phrase come from, anyhow?" asked Bryce. "'Lost in the shuffle.' Vegas? That's an idiom, like 'piece of cake.' What's so easy about cake?"

Carl spoke up. "In Japan, the equivalent phrase is 'before breakfast.'"

"At least that makes sense," Bryce admitted. "If something is easy, you can get it done before breakfast. Cakes, they need time to bake, you know, so they can ... uh ..."

"Rise," volunteered Myrtle. "Cakes need time to rise."

"Like bread," added Steely Slash Rab. "Unless it's unleavened, like at Passover."

"Now, Passover, that's a sensible name, too," continued Carl. "The Angel of Death passed over the homes that were properly marked on the door. But I never knew what the derivation was for Easter."

"Because the sun rises in the east, maybe?" mused Steely Slash Rab. "And, you know, God's son was rising that morning?"

Bryce practically did a spit-take with his coffee. "I don't think the homonym between sun and son goes back to the original non-English derivation, folks."

"Settle down!" barked Felicity. "The original question was whether Minx should cut the last line of her poem about alienation in the workplace."

"Yes."

"No way."

"Sure."

"It's her poem."

"Which poem was that?"

"Well, Minx," said Felicity. "I guess there's no consensus on that line. "Do you have anything else to say before we move on to Harold's latest crime caper?"

"Uh, no." Minx bit her lower lip and looked down at the table. "Thanks, everyone."

"Okay, then. Harold's chapter on the burglary gone bad. Anyone?" She looked at Bryce. Bryce was always the first to criticize Harold. Everyone knew that. "Remember. Sandwich critique method."

"Uh, oh, yeah," stuttered Bryce, obviously flailing for positive words. "I mean, it's cleanly written and technically fine, but there's no real suspense in it. You know? I mean, if the chapter is going to be compelling, there needs to be a better motive than petty theft. That and an identifiable bad guy for the reader to suspect—not just some anonymous stranger or strangers. And, since we don't really get to know the victims beforehand, there's no real sense of outrage over the crime or even a sense of loss. Unidentified strangers killing faceless strangers. It's like those giant robots killing other giant robots ..."

"Autobots and Decepticons," volunteered Steely Slash Rab. "Transformers. I ... uh ... saw the commercials."

"Yeah, what he said," continued Bryce. "There's no dramatic tension to the scene."

"What do you think, Gantry?" asked Felicity, looking at Gantry Ellis. "I mean, you're the expert in the group on crime fiction."

Gantry leaned forward in his chair. "Well, Bryce is right that it's not only important in a thriller to have a protagonist the reader either likes or, at least, can identify with, maybe even root for, but an antagonist which is sufficiently concrete and identifiable that the reader can focus their antagonism upon. That's why shadowy conspiracies with diffuse, ephemeral organizations as the big bad are dissatisfying to many readers. A large organization like the government or the mafia can't be killed or taken down, but an individual running that organization, or doing dirty deeds for it, makes a better target for the hatred of the reader. If the reader doesn't have someone clear to hate, they may focus their hatred on the book, itself, and you sure don't want that."

"Or they might focus their ... lack of enthusiasm ... on the author," said Bryce. "That's what I do."

Felicity slapped her notebook on the table. "No comments about the author, Bryce. That's not fair play."

"Speaking of fair play," interjected Myrtle, "how's the reader supposed to figure out who did the murders if they're just random killings by faceless punks? Seems like that would be frustrating to the reader ..."

Harold gritted his teeth. No, frustration was taking writing advice from someone who was nearly three hundred thousand words, and more than two hundred different fantasy characters, into a novel that had no discernible plot. He closed his eyes and fantasized for a moment about striding into the meadow world of Myrtle's dragonfly-mounted faeries and revving up his weed-whacker to slaughter the whole bunch of them. Now there would be a big bad everyone could identify with.

Carl jumped on the bandwagon. "Myrtle's got a point. A mystery's got to play fair on clues to the reader ..."

"It's not a fair-play mystery!" Harold shouted out. "It's a gritty, urban procedural. And this scene isn't the focus of the book. It's just there for atmosphere, to get the reader to appreciate the type of neighborhood it is, that the neighborhood is changing."

"Harold," snapped Felicity, "you know the author's not supposed to ..."

"Racial conflict is always good for an urban crime setting," interjected Gantry, "especially in a changing neighborhood. Pick your ethnicity and do your research. For instance, a lot of Korean bodegas opened up in black neighborhoods, but some of the locals resented the prices and the relative prosperity of the Koreans. Led to lots of armed robberies. And the animosity between rival gangs—black, Latino, Russian, Chinese, Vietnamese—that stuff fuels the big city crime statistics so much that some crime gets overlooked just to keep the numbers down. I left some notes on my mark-up."

"Oh, that's good," interrupted Steely Slash Rab. "A changing neighborhood has all sorts of gritty possibilities. Not just race conflict. Deteriorating housing values. Increasing crime. The claustrophobia of being afraid to open your own door, afraid of the gangbangers outside, confused by what the neighborhood is becoming, but trapped by the depressed real estate prices caused by materialistic, fat-cat investment bankers in their wealthy waterfront enclaves. All the pain and anguish of the 'hood can be artistically visualized by the amount and nature of the street art, because that's the only thing that's genuine, that's real." He looked around at the group. "Truth."

"Street art?" growled Carl. "Is that what you call that gang graffiti crap? Anybody try to tag my house, they're going to get a double-barrel of rock salt in their ass, right before I reach for the double-aught buckshot shells."

"Enough!" shouted Felicity. "I think we've gotten a bit off-topic." She turned her face toward Harold. "It's the author's turn to speak. Harold? Anything to say in response?"

Ethnic animosity. Gang violence. Graffiti. No, he had everything he needed now, thanks to the always dysfunctional PMWGCS. He smiled. "No, Felicity. Thanks, everyone, for your comments. They've given me a lot of good ideas."

#

Guy flipped through Sweater Vest's scenario. "I dunno. Pissin' off a street gang seems counter-productive to me. They got lookouts every whichway on their turf. You try to pin a crime on them, they're likely to come at you or have cold, hard facts they leak to the police."

"Read carefully," Sweater Vest replied, after yet another fucking eye-roll. "You're not pinning anything on the gang. I'm not asking you to tag a gang sign on the wall behind the bodies. You just want to hint that the crime may be related to the changing neighborhood. Look, it's a Polish couple ..."

"Czech."

"And the neighborhood, it's increasingly black and Latino, right?" Sweater Vest wriggled his fingers for a moment while he thought. "So just bust up anything obviously ethnic in the place."

"Obviously ethnic?"

Sweater Vest nodded enthusiastically. "Yeah, like ripping up any pictures of the old country or calendars or books not in English. You know, maybe stomping on any little Polish flags they have ..."

"Czech."

"Roger that."

"No, you idiot. Czech, like in The Czech Republic ... part of what used to be Czechoslovakia. They're not Polish, they're Czech."

Sweater Vest huffed and stared at him for a few seconds. "Many blacks and Latinos in the Czechopollock Republic?" He didn't wait for an answer. "Then it doesn't fucking matter. They're foreigners, right? How hard can it be to just hate 'em no matter where they're from? Break their jars of sauerkraut or drape sausages around their necks after they're dead. It doesn't matter. It doesn't have to make sense to you, it just has to suggest a motive to the police. That distracts the attention from the possibility of a professional hit. *Capiche?*"

"That's fucking Italian."

"So? You've said it to me."

"That's right. I can say things you can't. That's how this relationship works. First rule, you don't piss off your boss. Trust me, you don't want to start insulting Italians." He let that sink in for a moment, before continuing. "But, yeah, I understand."

He swore that Sweater Vest was even paler than usual, as if that were possible. The scribe gulped, then simply said, "I understand, too."

Maybe he should have told his co-conspirator that Guy was an Americanized nickname for Guido.

Nah.

Having a grown man piss his pants in public tends to draw unwanted attention.

Chapter 12

His local paper was, of course, of no use whatsoever in tracking whether there had been a murder in some lower-class neighborhood in the city. Suburbanites didn't want to read about that. So Harold was forced to log on to the Crime Beat page for the city daily and search for "murder." Nothing yet on the latest job, but he did pick up an update on the sister-kills-wealthier-brother frame-up. Sis had been arrested and, later, released on bail after the brother's family put up the money for her bond. She'd used her freedom pending trial to commit suicide with five bottles of over-the-counter sleeping pills washed down with a fifth of marshmallow vodka.

S'more, the merrier.

He couldn't help but smile. It's not that he wanted the sister to die. Hell, he didn't know her, had never met her. Reading about her dying was like reading about some Darwin Award winner ganking himself by using a shotgun shell as a handy replacement when he ran out of fuses for the house's electrical box. Evolution in action, man. It had no more effect on him than reading about tsunami victims or Venezuelan protesters or Nigerian tribesmen dying in droves. The world had too many people anyhow.

No, the only difference was that this death, this suicide, proved he was a great writer. He had written a plot scenario so clever, so credible, so emotionally wrenching that she willingly gave her life up in response to it. That was the ultimate review, better than any given by the trolls and wannabes on Goodreads or Amazon. This was *New York Times*, *Kirkus*, and *Publisher's Weekly* all rolled into one.

This was a big "Fuck You!" to everyone in the PMWGCS, especially that asshole, Bryce. Could even Gantry Ellis say someone had given their life for his writing? He didn't think so.

No, he ... not Gantry, not Bryce or Carl or Bob Steely Slash fucking Rab, and certainly not any of the women ... was the best writer in the PMWGCS. He couldn't tell them, of course. They would never know. After all, they'd never recognized his genius before.

But he knew. And, for today, that was enough.

#

"So, did you get all the information you needed from my guy?"

Gantry Ellis frowned and he closed his eyes tight, trying his best to remember which of the hundreds of contacts and referrals he connected with during his research for the Danger McAdams series had come from the fellow on the phone.

No luck.

"Ahhh, sorry, Frank. Which information are you referring to? My plate's pretty full these days."

Frank's voice grew softer, as if the NSA couldn't just turn up the volume if they were listening. "You know, the friend of the friend ... the hit man. I called in a marker for you; he promised he'd have a sit-down. Give you the real deal story and all."

Oh, the no-show he sent Harold to meet. Now he remembered. Still, it wouldn't do to not be grateful for the contact, even if it didn't pan out. Embarrassing a contact was a sure way to lose him. "Oh, yeah, Frankie. Can't say more. Promised it was all hush-hush, you know. But, rest assured I got what I needed. I'll send you a copy of my next book, personalized as usual."

Gantry knew Frank had no interest in his autograph or, more accurately, the Cain Abel signature he used for autographing books. But Frank did like the hundred dollar bill Gantry tucked inside the pages of copies he sent to confidential sources who helped him with research. It wasn't Frank's fault the guy didn't follow through, after all. Sure, maybe Frank was scamming him, but he didn't think so. Besides, it was a business expense, so the government was footing half the bill—heck, more than half if you counted state income tax—just like it footed half the bill for every trip he took these days. All for research, of course.

God Bless America.

#

Guy used a couple of two-liter plastic pop bottles as makeshift silencers, one for each victim, just as Sweater Vest had advised, because that's what an amateur killer would do. It was messy—bits of plastic flying about—and not completely effective, but this wasn't the kind of neighborhood where people paid too much mind to popping noises in the night, especially when muffled enough to sound like they were not that close. Besides, this was also the kind of neighborhood where police response was not that quick ... or even sure ... when the cops were called.

As he wandered through the place looking for items that were "obviously ethnic" to destroy, he wondered idly for a moment what this middle-aged Czech couple could have done to make someone willing to pay his fee to eliminate them. It's not like they had any money. Maybe it was retaliation for something back in Eastern Europe. Religious and political factions could be more ruthless than gangbangers; they certainly had longer memories. His eyes fell upon some old china plates hanging on the dining room wall next to the hutch.

103

Keepsakes from the old country?

Close enough. He smashed them with the butt of his gun.

He found a menu in the kitchen for the local delicatessen and ripped it up, scattering the pieces in the still growing pools of blood next to his targets. It felt cheesy and theatrical, but Sweater Vest was right when he said the police seized on cheesy, theatrical clues, especially when they didn't have any real forensics. Of course, they might have some of that, too. On Sweater Vest's recommendation, he had also grabbed a few pieces of "evidence" from the street as he strode toward the apartment. Nothing much, just a couple of cigarette butts. He scattered the butts near the door, as if someone had been lying in wait before breaking in and killing the couple and taking their cash and meager valuables.

He'd dump the valuables as soon as possible, but if he was going to fake a burglary or at least fake faking a burglary, he needed to go through the motions. The cash, he'd keep, as long as it wasn't bloodstained. He was going through extra effort on these hits since he teamed up with Sweater Vest. He didn't mind a bit of money to cover the extra overhead, not that Sweater Vest was getting paid that much.

Writers. They'd give away their work product for free if you gave 'em half a chance.

#

Harold's earlier flush of excitement from reading about the sister's suicide from his second writing assignment made him eager to find more "reviews," but Guy's rant a few weeks ago about his attendance at that target's funeral cooled Harold's enthusiasm for making personal contact. Instead he surfed the net, using the indices on several news websites to check for developments. When those efforts revealed nothing fresh on that case, he circled back to the carbon monoxide death he had engineered for his first assignment, switching over to Boolean search strings on Google.

A few keystrokes and a bit of scrolling and perusing led him to the widow's—Connie's—Facebook page. He sent a friend request, mentioning he had met her husband through business some years earlier, but had only recently learned of his death. By the next morning, Harold was a bit surprised to find she had accepted his invite—people in mourning find it difficult to be suspicious of expressions of condolence, he guessed. Postings were sparse for the next few days—mostly other people posting condolences and asking what they could do to help, or recommending a book or a therapist or a vacation. But later, on the third night, Connie posted a bit of a rant.

#

The Coroner finalized his ruling this afternoon that Rob's death was a suicide, even though I know in my heart that it was just a stupid accident. I've explained to the police and everyone that Rob wasn't suicidal, that he wouldn't ever do such a thing to me or the kids, but they just won't listen. The Coroner cited a report from the forensics team suggesting that the garage had been sealed up tight as an indication that Rob made a deliberate effort to keep the carbon monoxide in the car's exhaust from escaping, so it would rise rapidly to toxic levels. The place was drafty, that's all, and Rob was probably just being cheap about heat, what with last winter being so cold. Either that or he saw another mouse. He was always more scared of them than I was.

All of this would be meaningless, bureaucratic nonsense, but not even two hours passed after the Coroner's ruling when the insurance company called and said not only were they not paying the double indemnity for accidental death, but they were denying the claim outright because the death was self-inflicted and there's a suicide exception. I don't know what we're going to do. I mean, we got a little bit from Rob's 401(k) and the family's health insurance can be continued for a while, but without the life insurance, there's no way we'll be able to keep the house.

The silver lining, I guess, is that I can't bring myself to go into the garage, so we were probably going to have to move anyway, but we've got no equity and without the insurance there's no way we can make the down payment for a new house, even a smaller one.

#

The posting had been removed by the next day, Harold noticed, but that didn't matter to him. He'd printed it out when he first saw it, a memento of another writing success.

The cops, the Coroner, the insurance company, they all danced to his tune. They all played in his world now, a world of imagination and murder. Gantry Ellis and his Danger McAdams stories were just that, stories. Harold was the real Cain Abel now—the master of murder, the wordsmith of death.

#

A few weeks later, Harold had yet another assignment from Guy. He couldn't have been more excited. This one was a celebrity. Okay, a minor celebrity from a basic cable TV reality show called *Love Shack-les*, where the contestants, male and female, were shackled to a counterpart while they went on "dates" to various clubs, restaurants, bars, and art & entertainment venues, scoring points for doing various activities from bowling to dancing to feeding each other messy foodstuffs to engaging in over-the-top ... and under-the-top ... public displays of affection. Every week, the couples were separated and re-shackled to new counterparts/contestants. Lower budget and sleazier than network fare like *The Bachelor*, the stupid stunts, skimpy clothing, and outrageous character conflicts gave the show a train-wreck quality that garnered it a following in the 18-30 year-old demographic. Now, someone apparently wanted one of the women dead and was willing to pay for it.

Harold got busy on his keyboard. A few trashy tabloid sites later, he discovered that his target had a stalker. Cops loved stalkers. He quickly wrote up a few pages, changing a few key facts and formatting it to look like a segment of a larger work so he could turn it in the PMWGCS on Saturday for fleshing out.

Sometimes things just came easy.

#

"This is just too easy," whined Bryce ten days later. "I mean, it's just too obvious. The cops will always look at the stalker of a celebrity. Where's the suspense?"

"A good twist," cooed Myrtle, "that's what I look for in a mystery—a twist. You know, like identical twins or a dagger made out of ice, or the killer being an ex-boyfriend presumed dead in a mountain-climbing expedition."

Felicity nodded. "Which would be why he would know how to make a proper ice dagger."

"No, no," said Steely Slash Rab, with a shake of his head. "That's like, I dunno, the kind of twist you get on a soap opera. Harold's aiming higher than that I think."

"You think Hack aims at something when he's flailing about on the keyboard?" asked Bryce.

"A twist is good," agreed Carl, "as long as it's properly foreshadowed. None of that introducing a new character in the last ten pages who ends up being the killer, crap. I read something like that, I throw the book across the room and vow never to read the author again."

Gantry nodded. "You can't maintain a stable fandom if too many of your readers do that too often."

"Besides," complained Steely Slash Rab. "A love-struck, lonely guy as the killer is just too cliché. You don't want to do that."

Harold said nothing, but rolled his eyes. Gee, Bob, hitting a little too close to home?

Minx spoke up, albeit in a quiet voice. "Maybe ..."

Harold heard her, but the group rolled on, arguing about the merits of soap opera twists versus the foreshadowing on procedural shows. She raised her hand and waited. Finally, Felicity saw her.

"Yes, dear?"

"Maybe," said Minx quietly. "Maybe the girl's ex-boyfriend from like high school or something, he regrets dumping her now that she's famous and he gets his revenge by killing her and framing the stalker."

"Now that's a plot," rumbled Gantry. "If the stalker is truly watching the victim almost all the time, it would be easy for someone low profile, like an ex-boyfriend, to identify him and set him up. The real killer could gather up some food wrappers with his DNA, maybe snag a note he'd written to her, or get some fibers or hair or something. A low key chat with the guy might even dislodge a fetish or fantasy the stalker has which the ex-boyfriend could use to frame him as the murderer. I like it."

Harold smiled. He liked it, too.

Chapter 13

"What?" grumbled Guy. "Now I'm framing someone who is attempting to frame someone else? How many layers are we going to go on this shit? It's a whole lot more work than two-in-the-back-of-the-head, you know. My life got a shitload more complicated when I started working with you, and it ain't just because of all these meetings in the park."

"Look," replied Sweater Vest with a huff, "you come to me, you get a quality product. The best frame is a frame that's done by somebody else. You get twice the protection here, for only a little more effort. If the cops are lazy, they finger the stalker and you're in the clear. If they put down their doughnuts and push a bit harder 'cause they're bucking for a promotion or whatever, and they look through the frame, then they collar the old ex-boyfriend and you're still in the clear."

Guy thought for a minute. "How'd you find the ex-boyfriend, anyhow?"

Sweater Vest tilted his head, probably so he could look down his nose better at Guy. "High school yearbook. It's amazing what you can get online these days. And, of course, because I looked it up, not you, you're in the clear should any suspicion ever fall on you. Your browser history is clean."

Guy smiled. "My browser history's filthy, but I get your drift." He skimmed through Sweater Vest's plotline one more time. "Rest of it looks pretty straightforward. I'll check in with the friend of the friend of the customer and go forward on this basis, assuming there's no problem."

Sweater Vest jerked in alarm. "Check in? I work for you. I don't want anyone else second-guessing my work. I don't need critics, especially amateurs."

"Don't get your panties twisted, my contact knows nothing about you. He's got no reason to know, so he doesn't. Period."

"Then why do you have to check in?"

Guy sighed. "You do understand that the core concept of a frame is that someone besides me gets blamed for the murder, right?"

"I'm sure my vocabulary is much more extensive than yours."

"Fine. Then maybe, just maybe, before I go pinning this job on somebody else you picked out of the blue ... or the world wide web ... I should make sure the person I'm framing *and* the person I'm setting up to look like he's framing the guy I'm framing, aren't, you know, the actual client here. Blaming the guy who's a friend of my friend who set this all up is not conducive to my future business prospects. Nor would it be conducive to walking away from this job without complications. Understood?"

"I guess that makes sense."

"It does. Trust me. You, my friend, have given me the names of the stalker and the ex-boyfriend. I simply make a call and make sure they aren't the ultimate customer, that's all. Then, if I'm in the clear, I start following your suggestions for setting them both up."

"According to the inscriptions in the yearbook copy online, the ex-boyfriend's nickname back in the day was Kip, so if you connect in any way with the stalker or want to leave an extra hint about the ex-boyfriend, use the name Kip. It'll throw suspicion his way if anybody gets that far down the trail."

"This Kip, is he my evil twin or something?"

"Same color hair, medium build. It's more than a decade later and people are crap at describing people they've barely met, so you're close enough on looks it might not hurt."

"Especially if I wear shades and a baseball cap. What's the nearest major league team to where these young lovers did the deed after prom?"

Sweater Vest glanced at his notes. "Chicago."

"So, Cubs or White Sox?"

"Cubs."

"Fifty-fifty guess?" Guy liked confidence, but Sweater Vest was getting cocky.

"Suburban high school, northwest side. Gotta be Cubs. The fan base market reach of the White Sox barely gets out of the few blocks surrounding the field on the South Side of Chicago."

"So says a suburbanite."

Sweater Vest looked at Guy with half-lidded eyes. "There was a map making the rounds on Facebook."

Guy chuckled. "Don't believe everything you read on the internet, kid. If you knew my name and looked me up, it would say I was rep for a beer distributor."

Sweater Vest shrugged. "So, you don't really distribute beer?"

Guy smiled. "Just from the bottle to the toilet, with stops at my mouth, throat, stomach, and bladder along the way."

#

No need to scan the inside pages of the Local or Metro sections this time. The murder of even a minor celebrity from cable TV made for a splashy "Dying to be on Television" headline on the front page of the Entertainment section and generated enough tweeting and posting that Harold could monitor details of the investigation by feed, rather than having to risk ferreting out information, himself.

He wasn't surprised when the cops arrested the stalker, but he was quite taken aback when the stalker ended up making a full confession and insisting on the death penalty—no luck there, since the state had a moratorium on executions. Apparently, once the loser got some media attention, he was more enamored with being known as the killer of his celebrity crush and joining her in eternity, than in falling back into obscurity with a side of microwaved ramen noodles in an empty apartment.

Even though his plan had worked and his client was in the clear due to his research and plotline, Harold was disappointed at the result. It's not that he had anything in for the ex-boyfriend, but that whole layer of plotting ended up wasted. Of course, Guy knew he was smart and creative and all, but nobody else even knew about his clever twist. It was worse than ghostwriting. Sure, when you ghostwrote, nobody but you and a few editors and contract people at the publishing house knew you had written the book published under a pen name, but at least people got to see the work. You could monitor sales, not that ghostwriters usually got paid extra above the flat work-for-hire rate, and read reviews which talked about how clever the plot and great the dialogue was. Here, it was like masturbating. A few moments of vivid fantasy focused on your own awesome prowess and an appreciative audience, followed by a lifetime of loneliness, regret, and despair.

Only Guy and the members of the PMWGCS even knew of the extra plot layer ... and the dweebs at the PMWGCS didn't *really* know how clever he was. They only saw, would ever see, his first draft. They'd never see the final, polished, revised plotline in action in the real world.

He felt cheated.

#

"You been cheating on us, Hack?" asked Bryce as the next meeting of the PMWGCS gathered at the township hall. "And here I thought you were monogamous; celibate, bordering on impotent."

Harold eyed Bryce with even more than usual disgust. "Whatever are you talking about?"

Bryce dangled a printout of a newspaper article in front of him. "Stumbled on this in the library, when I was looking up an article about a Civil War re-enactment at the Historical Society's museum grounds a few weeks back. Says some lady was arrested for killing her brother. Police suspect incest as the motive."

Harold shrugged. "That's ... uh ... quite a coincidence."

Bryce gave him an odd stare. "I think both you and me, we know it's more than that."

Harold could feel the blood draining from his face. "We do?"

"We do," Bryce nodded. "I gotta confess, at first I just figured you were a plagiarist."

That last word silenced all of the chitchat in the rest of the room. Everyone turned to look at the two of them; Gantry Ellis even moved toward them, perhaps ready to forestall a physical confrontation. As Harold took in the scene, the faces of his colleagues ranging from shocked to accusatory, he felt the drained blood rush back in, flushing his face as his hands involuntarily tightened into fists. "Now, just one damn minute ..."

Bryce held up his hands in surrender. "But then I realized I was wrong. The events post-dated the meeting when we discussed your mystery thriller scene. So I figured, well, truth is stranger than fiction, and, in your case, the truth is better written, too, even though you have lately improved somewhat from your usual pathetic pussy police patrol patter. And that's when it hit me; that's when I realized you were two-timing the group."

What the fuck? "I have no idea what you're talking about," answered Harold.

"Here's how I figure it," explained Bryce. "You get ... or steal ... some idea for a story line and you write it up and take it to some writers group. Not here, though. Maybe online or in Napier or Colville or Ashbury. And you submit it and get comments from other people, people with better ideas than you. And then you polish it up and submit it to another group, maybe ours. Then get even better comments and polish it up even more and submit it to another group and another and maybe another, 'til you submit it somewhere where people actually like it because it's not half bad." Bryce shrugged. "The way I map it out, you probably have six, seven groups you attend. After all, it's not like they're going to interfere with your social life."

Gantry intervened. "Now, see here, Bryce. That's about enough. Hear? Enough."

Harold closed his eyes tight, pursing his lips and shaking his head as he tried to sort out Bryce's accusation. His tormentor was being insulting, as usual, but he wasn't even making any sense. He should have let it drop, now that Gantry had come to his defense, but he couldn't let it go. "How ... Even if any of that were true, how does that explain the newspaper article? It's just a coincidence. I'm sure pedophile and incest victims murder their attackers all the time."

"Less vigilante justice against pedophiles than you might think, elsewise there'd be a lot less Catholic priests." Bryce waved away the issue. "The point is that someone in one of your other groups, maybe they got inspired by the story. Decided to take matters into their own hands or maybe somebody cruising the mystery writer groups looking for ideas fixated onto this one as a way to throw suspicion on somebody else. You should revise your résumé, dude, and add 'Accessory before the Fact.'"

"Fuck you, Bryce," growled Harold as he made an abrupt about-face and headed toward the door.

"Now, now, gentleman," cooed Felicity. "I think that's quite enough, too."

Harold turned his body as he kept stomping toward the exit and raised his right hand, giving Felicity, Bryce, all of them, the finger. "Make your own damn coffee," he yelled as he burst through the door. "I hope you all choke on it."

He reached into his pocket for his car keys and instead found the Township's spare key. He flung it as far away as he could as he continued to fume. Bryce thought himself clever and cute, but he was just jealous. They were all jealous. Well, he didn't need them. He'd never really needed—certainly had never heeded—their advice. They'd just been an audience, but he didn't need them as an audience anymore.

The world was his audience now and it danced to his words, even if it never knew he wrote them.

He'd written a hit, four of them now. All he had to do was keep churning out the sequels and he was set for life.

Chapter 14

Gantry was a solid researcher. On top of that, he had plenty of contacts in law enforcement all across the country. He'd picked up a fair bit of information about detective work along the way, interesting tidbits of data about DNA and trace evidence, forensics and forensic counter-measures, interrogation techniques, and legal technicalities and limitations. He knew the lingo and the atmosphere, the dark underside to both the city and those who protected it, and what to do to fight dirty. But, despite all that, he wasn't a detective.

Yet, here he was, trying to figure out if someone he knew—someone he had befriended, tried to help out—was a murderer. Whether he, Gantry Ellis, had inadvertently caused a homicide.

He'd long ago come to grips with the fact that some arcane piece of information in one of his stories might be used by a stranger to help get away with a crime. Mimicry as flattery wasn't limited to the written word. But that was all part and parcel of writing about crime. Criminals were, for the most part, stupid and stupider. But, stupid criminals weren't entertaining to readers; readers demanded clever criminals. And by meeting the public demand for smart criminals and sophisticated techniques, you always took the chance that bad guys would pick up on something in your work. Like most stupid people, stupid criminals took their education where they found it, rather than actively seeking to better themselves. How many criminals had gotten away with a crime because of something they learned on *CSI*, *Law & Order*, or *NYPD Blue*? He shuddered to think. Certainly hundreds, if not thousands. Even if they hadn't copied crime techniques, countless perps, thugs, unsubs, and skels had had the Miranda warning beaten into their heads over their lifetime of television viewing, enough to make them ask for a lawyer rather than falling for good-cop, bad-cop routines.

This, though, this was different. He was playing detective, trying to solve a crime, maybe multiple crimes. Crimes that he not only may have set in motion, but crimes which he ... and the other members of the PMWGCS had helped plot and polish.

Bryce's newspaper article had slammed against Frank's follow-up call in the neurons of Gantry's brain. Maybe it was all coincidence. Maybe he'd spent so much time imagining murder and mayhem, he couldn't help but think dark, wild thoughts, but he had to see it through.

He had three crimes to research: the incest-motivated killing of a brother, allegedly by a sister who had later committed suicide; a supposedly ethnically motivated double homicide in a high-crime neighborhood; and a celebrity stalker case. He prayed there weren't others.

He set aside the cat mystery. If a cat could solve a crime, he figured real detectives would tumble across that perpetrator without his help.

He devoured all the information he could find on the incest case, then called some confidential contacts and pressed for any additional detail he could get. The more details he got, the worse he felt about the whole situation. The minutiae, the kind of stuff reporters didn't care about or the police never reported in order to be able to tell real criminals from psychotic wannabes, all lined up with the group's comments or were mere extrapolations. Worse yet, some of the minor details came from comments Gantry, himself, had made as marginal notes on the copy of Ackerman's draft he had returned at the end of the session—the group members always marked and returned drafts they reviewed so the group didn't get bogged down in copyedit comments and so even those too timid to criticize in public were able to communicate their thoughts to the author in private.

He pressed on immediately to researching the racially motivated ersatz burglary gone bad, ignoring his looming deadline on his Danger McAdams draft and canceling a scheduled book signing fifty miles away.

By the time he finished the "burglary" research, dawn was almost upon him and he felt physically ill, not from lack of food or sleep, but from what he had inadvertently wrought. There was no mistaking the fingerprints of the PMWGCS all over the crime scene for the double homicide in the city. Worse yet, in the midst of his "burglary" research, he had tumbled across the details of a recent minor-celebrity apparently murdered by a deranged stalker—the splashy death of someone even remotely famous always took precedence over the deaths of hard-working decent folks in the minds of the press.

Harold J. Ackerman's involvement in three real-life murders was clear to him, though he knew he would have a tough time selling the theory to the authorities, especially since he strongly suspected Harold had not committed the crimes personally. Harold could easily have rock-solid alibis for each of the various times of death.

He needed to gather more information. He needed to goad Harold into saying too much ... in public, with witnesses. God help him, he needed Harold to return to the PMWGCS. And for that, he needed some cooperation.

#

"Apologize," barked Gantry.

Bryce snorted. "Apologize to Hack? You've got to be shitting me. His writing belongs at the bottom of a litter box and his personality is what gets scooped out of one. What'd he do? Go whining to his mentor that big, bad Bryce said unkind things about his writing? He needs to deal with reality. In the unlikely event any of the crap he writes ever does get published, he'll get a lot worse from reviewers. Sure, Amazon filters out the bad language, but reviews can be tough. The Goodreads crowd is even tougher."

"No, he didn't ask me to call ..."

"Jesus," Bryce whined. "Don't tell me Felicity called and asked you to talk with me. The power of being de facto facilitator must be going to her head. The group would be more harmonious if Hack never came back. The average quality of the writing and the conversation would both go through the roof. I, frankly, don't care if he never comes back."

"I do," growled Gantry. "It's more important than you know."

"Look, Gantry, I know you've kinda taken Hack under your wing and all, but, trust me, you can do better. I wouldn't think a guy with your profile wants a needy little groupie like him. And if you do, do it on your own time. There's no reason to inflict him on the group."

"You're wrong," snapped Gantry. "There's a very important reason to get him to come back to the group ... a life-and-death reason."

"This I gotta hear ..."

"You were right. Don't you get it? You were right that someone is committing real crimes based off of Harold's stories, but I don't think it's someone from another group."

"Well, it ain't Hack. His writing may be pain-inducing, but I can't see him competently executing an execution."

"No, not Harold."

"Then who? It's not me and I doubt you would have made this call if it was you. So who does that leave? Felicity and Myrtle playing *Arsenic and Old Lace* with an assist from Pilkington? Bob getting so into his gangsta Steely Slash Rab persona, he's started murdering on the sly 'cause he doesn't have a car to pop rival thugs in a drive-by? Minx ... Minx is no danger to anybody, except maybe herself."

"No. No one from the group. I think he's choreographing murders for a hit man, running a frame shop out of the PMWGCS."

Bryce laughed out loud. "Dude, you need to take a break from the pulp drama of Danger McAdams. Hack's idea of social interaction is forwarding a Facebook meme to all twelve of his 'friends.' If he interacts with anyone face-to-face, it's at a cat mystery convention or, God help us, the PMWGCS. How would nebbishy little Hack hook up with a hit man? Couldn't happen, not in a million years."

"It could," murmured Gantry. "Y'see ... I think I might have introduced them to each other."

"You what? Why the hell would you ever do something like that?"

"It wasn't really intentional ..." Gantry sighed. He wished that was true, but it really wasn't. He had to live up to his responsibility for the situation eventually ... even to the authorities. He might as well start here. "Well, it sorta was, but just to interview him, if the hit man showed at all, as background research. I thought it was a wild goose chase and Harold seemed like a fellow with time on his hands, one who probably wouldn't mind a little spare cash for helping another writer out. So I sent him off to the meet, but Harold said the guy never showed. I thought nothing more of it at the time, but now ..."

"Now," replied Bryce. "Now you think they're working together. You've created a monster ... and you don't know how to stop him."

"Yes and no," said Gantry, with a shake of his head. "I'm mighty fearsome about what I may have set in motion, but I have an inkling of how to stop things."

"How?"

"First off, you need to apologize to Harold. That way, he'll come back to the group."

"What's that going to do? We can't just wait to see what lame-ass crime scene he has this week, help him out with it, and wait for more people to die in order to confirm our suspicions and gather evidence. Helping Hack kill more people doesn't strike me as moral or effective."

"It is if we know the target and arrange for the cops to be waiting, ready to snatch him up."

Bryce barked out a laugh. "If wishes were horses, beggars would ride. Hack may be an incompetent writer, but he's not stupid enough to tell the PMWGCS who the target is and when they'll be hit. He may not even know all those details. If I was a hit man, I wouldn't trust a dweeb like Hack any further than he would be blown back if hit by a discharging blunderbuss."

"That's why we have to take *complete* control of the situation ..."

Chapter 15

Harold didn't pull into the parking lot of the Township Offices until a few minutes past 10:00 a.m. on Saturday. Bryce had had to do a lot of apologizing and convincing, and then some more apologizing, to get Harold to return to the group. Harold certainly wasn't going to come back as a subservient little schlep who unlocked the door, set up the chairs, and started coffee. No, if he was coming back to the PMWGCS, it was as a treasured guest and respected resource for the various amateurs in the group. He hadn't even brought anything along for the group to critique at its next session. He didn't have a new project yet from Guy and, besides, he preferred to make the PMWGCS members beg to see his writing again, whining like they always did when Gantry Ellis failed to bring a new chapter for review.

The group fell silent as he walked in the door. He stopped and simply stood there.

Finally, Felicity spoke up. "Harold ... I didn't expect to see you again ... I mean, today."

Gantry smiled at him. Minx looked at the tabletop. Pilkington's eyes scanned over Harold's body, as if searching for the outlines of a concealed weapon. Myrtle's face remained frozen, as her eyes darted about, apparently gauging the reaction of others. Steely Slash Rab's hands fluttered rapidly, either giving Harold a wave or attempting to flash gang signs—with Bob you could never be sure. Bryce stared straight at him, his eyes twitching with apprehension.

Felicity continued. "It's good to have you back."

Harold remained still, rather than moving toward his usual seat. "That remains to be seen, whether I'm actually back. It all depends." He turned his head toward Bryce. "Do you have something to say, Bryce?"

They'd worked this all out during Bryce's apology call, but Harold doubted Bryce would follow through. After all, he was an arrogant, little punk—a critic, not a real writer. Sure, he pounded out the epic Civil War quatrains with mechanical regularity, but it's not like poetry was real writing.

Real writers, like Harold, affected the real world.

"Yes, Ha...Harold," Bryce stammered. "I just want to tell you ... in front of everyone here ... that it was wrong and unprofessional of me to make completely unfounded accusations against you and to disparage you and your writing, both of which I admire and respect." He faltered for a moment, as if trying to remember the correct words to his rehearsed speech. "I greatly appreciate, as I'm sure everyone else here does, that you deign to participate in, and graciously contribute your considerable talents toward, the work and writing of the Pleasant Meadow Writers' Guild and Critiquing Society, and I ask that you continue to do so."

As Bryce talked, Harold took in the shocked expressions of the others, save Carl Pilkington, who fixed him with a steely stare, and Gantry, who simply nodded, as if in agreement. He would, of course, have preferred they all be nodding in agreement, even interrupting to voice their own pleas that he stay, but this tableau was sufficient, for now.

"Your apology and your invitation on behalf of the group are both accepted." Harold briskly walked to his usual place and sat. "Please proceed."

Felicity coughed twice, then seemed to settle herself. "Well, Harold, we were just starting to talk about Carl's latest chapter, about his exploits with an Army nurse in, what was it, Belgium, Luxembourg?

Felicity's question jarred Sergeant Pilkington out of his stare. "Correct on both counts, Miss Felicity. Nurse Ethel and I, we invented the modern travel itinerary. Four countries in five days ..."

Then Myrtle giggled and Minx smiled and everything went back to way it usually was, with one exception. Everyone respected Harold now, as well they should.

#

"It's about time," whined Sweater Vest as Guy approached him in the park. "You're late."

Guy shrugged. "So? You work for me, remember? You need to learn a little respect."

"Whatever ..." drawled Sweater Vest. "Just give me the info and let me do my thing, so you can do your thing ... oh ... *without being caught.*"

Guy didn't need to put up with this shit. Literally, he didn't need to put up with Sweater Vest at all. He'd never gotten caught in the old days, when it was a .22 to the back of the head. He could always go back to the tried and true. Besides, Sweater Vest was getting increasingly arrogant and reckless with each frame job. He didn't need a professional writer to tell him when to cut his losses and leave his colleague high and dry. This would be their last job together. He simply gritted his teeth for a moment, then relaxed as if he didn't have a care in the world.

Looking casual under stressful situations was an important attribute for a professional hitter. The best way not to get identified when fleeing the scene of a crime was to act as if you were simply walking to the store for a pack of cigarettes rather than fleeing the scene of a crime.

"Pretty straightforward stuff. Gal in the suburbs has a boyfriend who beats on her. I'm being paid to make sure the beat-downs stop due to the boyfriend being dead and all."

"So the girl hired you?"

Guy counted to ten. "Don't know. Don't care. Nobody in the business ever asks those questions, exceptin' to make sure they're not framing the client. Maybe the girl, she can't take it any longer. Maybe her father or her ex-boyfriend or her best friend or some random peeping Tom, they want it stopped. Don't know. Don't care." He handed Sweater Vest a page from a phone book, with a name and address circled. "That's all I got and all you need to know, except for two things."

Sweater Vest said nothing, but began tapping his foot after a few seconds.

"One, you only got two-and-a-half weeks."

Sweater Vest looked to the side, as if so unconcerned as to be bored. "I can work to a deadline."

"Yeah," responded Guy. "Two, the hit's gotta occur at a specific time, exactly twenty days from today."

His colleague's eyebrows lifted. "Why?"

Guy sucked on a tooth for a moment. "Not completely sure. Blah blah about the target being on an erratic schedule, but the client knowing they would be home alone and asleep that night. More likely, the client just wants to make sure to have a clean alibi, maybe out of state. Me, I don't like these kinds of limitations. Cramps my style. You know, limits my flexibility and, of course, makes it easier for someone to set me up, but the pay is good and my source vouches the limitation is legit, so I'm playing along."

"Right."

"That means you gotta play along, too. No whack-a-doodle plans that depend on weather or television show schedules or any of that. Just do your research and tell me, soon as you can, who the fall guy is gonna be so I can make sure he's not the one paying for this little exercise. Are we clear?"

"Clear."

"I'll meet you here, same time, sixteen days from now."

"Fine."

Guy started to turn away.

Sweater Vest put his hand on Guy's shoulder. "There's just one other thing ..."

Guy resisted the instinctual urge to grab and fling somebody who had the sheer audacity to touch him. "What?" he growled, staring at the offending hand.

Sweater Vest let go. "We need to talk about my cut."

Of course the arrogant asshole wanted more money. Honor among thieves was a bullshit myth. Bad guys were always out for themselves. That's what made them bad guys. Well, Guy had turned the mild-mannered king of the dweebs, here, into a bad guy, so, of course, he was resorting to form. This just confirmed Guy's earlier decision. But, of course, there was no reason to reveal any of that now.

"I understand," said Guy. "To do that, though, I'll have to adjust my pricing. This deal's already done, but we can talk at the next meeting about a price adjustment going forward. In the meantime, think about whether you want a simple raise in the flat rate you're getting or if you want to go on a percentage basis. Just remember though, I've got the contacts and I take the risks, so don't get too greedy."

"This is a lot of work. I deserve a raise."

Guy put his hand on Sweater Vest's shoulder. "And you'll get one. Hell, kid, I respect you for asking for one. Most guys, they don't have the *cajonés* for that. You're coming up in the world, kid. Stick with me and one day you'll have it made."

He let the word "made" just hang there. He didn't mean anything by it, but let Sweater Vest imagine anything he wanted, if it would keep him in line for this job and keep his mouth shut going forward. Guy turned and left without saying "goodbye."

Just one more meeting and this relationship was over. And, like every other relationship in his life, he was the one ending it and he'd make sure the other party never saw it coming.

Chapter 16

He never saw that coming.

Harold sat bolt upright in his chair as he scrolled through the Facebook postings of the latest target, seeing a familiar face again and again and again.

Holy shit! The target was apparently Minx's current squeeze. It's not like there were love letters or any romantic bullshit like that in the postings, but the dude—Christoph—had his arm around her in several of the postings of his band at various gigs, and he could see the adoration in Minx's eyes, because it was all he ever dreamt for. And now, now he was being paid to save Minx from her asshole, abusive boyfriend.

This was just too good.

Harold wasn't the one who did the actual killing, of course. That dirty work was handled by Guy. But, with this situation, Harold had an opportunity to kill two birds with one stone and, when it was all over, wind up with the girl. Better yet, the second target would unknowingly assist in the set-up.

#

Bryce leaned forward at the PMWGCS meeting twelve days later, like a fanboy in the front row of the cosplay competition at ComiCon awaiting the parade of nearly naked female flesh mimicking gamer-geek heroines. Harold suppressed a smirk. Bryce spent years of his life studying Civil War battles, but like the South, had no idea he was facing an enemy with infinite patience and much greater resources.

Finally, Felicity turned to the next manuscript on her stack. "Any comments on the latest chapter in Harold's murder mystery series?"

"Yes, Felicity. I have a few things," blurted Bryce.

"Go ahead, but remember to say something positive ..."

Bryce fluttered his left hand at Felicity. "No problem. Hack ... er ... Harold does a great job here, setting up the female character realistically and sympathetically. You really get the impression she's in a tough place. I mean, she loves this guy, but he treats her like shit, and it's not that she doesn't realize it, but she believes in true love. And even if she didn't, she's got no real alternatives. I mean, she doesn't have a car or any money. It's a great set-up, but then, boom, near the end of a chapter this hit man shows up and, blam, it's two in the back of the head of the boyfriend with a .22. I mean, I suppose it's realistic in a way, but it doesn't have any finesse, any tension, any emotional payoff for the reader."

"I agree with Bryce," drawled Gantry. "Whenever there's a fight scene or violence, the action needs to be commensurate in length and detail to the set-up. Put simply, the more the reader has invested in the conflict, the longer and more vivid the actual resolution of that conflict needs to be. You don't spend a whole cowpoke story setting up a one-on-one gunfight at high noon and then just say one guy died when the clock strikes twelve. You gotta feel the hot, dry breeze blowin' tumbleweeds down the street as the two guys squint at one another, each waitin' to get and take whatever advantage they can. Time's gotta slow down for the fight ..."

"That's how it is, in real battles," concurred Carl. "The faster the lead is flying past your head, the slower time moves, 'til you can see and sense everything, from the smell of cordite to your tongue sticking to the roof of your dry mouth and the sweat stinging your eyes as you watch bullets—goddamn supersonic bullets—going in one side of your buddy's shoulder and coming out the other side with a shower of blood and muscle and cloth and flecks of bone while a cacophony of screams and explosions and whispered prayers float past your ears and mix in with your brain, threatening to devour your dreams and your soul." Carl's nose twitched and he grabbed a handkerchief to tend to a hovering drop of mucous, as well as take a surreptitious swipe at a tear-filled eye. "Folks only say 'It all happened so fast, 'cause when something like that occurs, there's no time to do anything to *stop* it, not because there ain't an eternity to take it all in, whether you want to or not."

There was an awkward moment of silence, then Myrtle reached over and squeezed Carl's hand. "Thank you for your service, Sergeant Pilkington. Thank you, so much."

"Thanks from us all," agreed Gantry. "As tough as that real life experience is, it's the job of a thriller author to convey that same level of detail and emotion. As for Harold's scene here, I suppose you could try to stretch out the details of the double-tap, execution style, to convey the ruthless coldness of the hit, but that's been done before in the great pulp novels. No, here I think you focus in on the details of the hit man approaching the residence, getting into the house, and then, maybe killing the guy in a way reminiscent of the crimes the target is accused of. You know, the hit man stalks the abuser, maybe watches him through the window, then simply knocks on the door and pretends to be somebody he's not, befriending the target, until the target lets his guard down, then, WHAM! The hit man grabs a bat ..."

"... or a fireplace poker," interjected Bryce.

"... and just goes apeshit crazy, beating the target until he's down on the ground in a fetal position, his arms covering his head, just trying to survive the onslaught."

"And all the time," continued Bryce, picking up for Gantry in a rush of words, "the hit man's saying stuff like 'I love you,' and 'this hurts me more than it hurts you,' and 'why do you make me do this?' And when the target is scared to death and just barely alive, the killer gets the target's cell phone and tells him he'll stop beating on him if the target makes a recording where he's pleading for his life, but pleads as if the person beating him is whoever the hit man wants to finger for the deed—like the girl's overprotective father or someone like that. And then, when he's dead, the hit man uses the victim's finger to write a few letters in blood on the floor, like a deathbed accusation. Then the hit man can simply wipe down the shaft of the bat or fireplace poker or whatever, then chuck the murder weapon in a culvert near the dad's house. When the cops investigate, dad is pegged for the whole thing."

"Man," murmured Steely Slash Rab, "that was just like in a movie."

Felicity and Myrtle looked at Bryce aghast. Minx's head was down and she was shaking as she dabbed at her teary eyes. Carl's brow was furrowed. Gantry, however, nodded approvingly as Bryce finished his rant with an enthusiastic flourish: "That's how you do a fucking hit and frame some other poor sap for the crime!"

There was another pause, this one longer.

Finally, Felicity shook her head, as if clearing her thoughts, and plastered a motherly smile back on her face. "Harold? Any comments?"

"I ... I agree with Gantry. I think Bryce is absolutely correct." Several heads jerked back in disbelief at Harold's statement, before he continued. "Thank you, Bryce. It's obvious you've thought a lot about this situation. Both the detail and the passion you have for the scene are evident. I'll do my best to incorporate every single piece of your vision into my work."

#

Guy grimaced. If he hadn't already decided to cut ties with Sweater Vest, this latest script would have done the trick. This was some sick shit. He did his best, however, to remain nonchalant and professional.

"You remember what I told you, right?"

Sweater Vest rolled his eyes. Guy was tired of the whole fucking eye-rolling thing. "Be specific," demanded Sweater Vest. "What are you asking me to recollect?"

"That part I said, way back in the beginning, about not getting my jollies out of 'inconveniencing' people."

"Sure. So?"

"So, you should check out whether they need any script-writers for *Psycho Maniac Killer 5*."

"What?"

"Never mind," replied Guy. "Look, this plotline seems pretty violent, even passionate. Worse than that, beating someone to death with a makeshift bludgeon seems unnecessarily risky. What if there isn't a good weapon or they fight back? I mean, beating a guy, that's slow, uncertain work to get to death. Couldn't I put two in the back of his head and then beat the crap out of the body? Sounds more pleasant and less risky to me, if you get my drift."

"No," snarled Sweater Vest. "The frame job depends on this looking like a spontaneous crime of passion. Besides, the Medical Examiner, he'll be able to tell if the beating is inflicted post-death. The wounds won't bleed as much if the heart isn't still furiously pumping away when the gut is punctured or the head is cracked open."

Guy sucked a tiny morsel of gristle out of his teeth from the Sausage McMuffin he'd had for brunch. "Yeah, that whole gushing blood thing is an issue, too. Assuming I don't get blinded by hot, arterial spray, I'm still gonna be splattered from head to toe with DNA evidence."

"So, just dump your clothes as soon as possible."

"That's only the half of it. Not only do I have to find a dependable way to destroy or dump the clothes, blood causes all sorts of problems. Footprints, tracking it into my car or, hell, even my place. And people, they see you with blood spray on you, they call 9-1-1 with no questions asked."

"No one's going to see you. You're the one who said this has to occur in the middle of the fucking night. Who's gonna see you in the suburbs in the middle of the night?"

Shit. He'd have to do this one in paper booties and hospital scrubs. He'd done it once or twice before, but it always made him feel like a crazed surgeon out of some slasher flick.

"Fine. Whatever. What's all this crap about writing 'B-R' on the floor with the target's bloody finger? And the cellphone thing? What if the target doesn't cooperate or records something incriminating? Who the fuck is Bruce?"

Sweater Vest's brow furrowed and his eyes narrowed in an instant. "That's Bryce, with a *Y*. Got that? There can be no mistakes about that."

"Okay. Bryce. Are you sure he doesn't spell it with an *I*? Sounds kinda prissy to me."

"Bryce is the perfect patsy. He knows the victim. He knows her boyfriend beats on her. And there'll be plenty of evidence that he planned the whole thing."

"How are you going to do that? And how can someone plan a spontaneous crime of passion?"

Sweater Vest smiled. "Exactly. That's why it's a perfect frame."

Guy smiled back, but he wasn't happy. He wasn't at all happy. He'd created a monster by working with Sweater Vest and it was clear now that no longer working with the crazed scribe wouldn't be enough. No, like all the monsters wreaking havoc across the annals of fiction, this one needed to be destroyed.

Fortunately, bullets are cheap.

Two rattling around Sweater Vest's skull would do the trick. After all, there was plenty of room up there. The kid had clearly lost his marbles.

Usually, of course, Guy was supplied with the information he needed to do a job; he didn't hit anyone on his own accord. An address and a name, maybe just a photo, was enough to set an inconveniencing in motion. Here, there was no need for a photo. And all he had to do was follow the wordsmith when he left the meet and he'd eventually get a home address ... and probably an I.D. should he ever need or want it. Sweater Vest was simultaneously too much of an amateur and too much of an arrogant prick to be careful about watching his six on the drive home.

Location, location, location. The mantra didn't just apply to real estate.

Late night, at the target's home, that was the routine—the m.o.—for Guy before Sweater Vest. It seemed fitting that hitting Sweater Vest at home would be the lead-off for Guy's return to routine, even if it would be with a twist.

Chapter 17

Guy ambled along the sidewalk, looking, he hoped, like just some insomniac out for a stroll in the middle of the night. No booties or hospital scrubs, just a pair of jeans, a dark golf shirt, and a windbreaker jacket. No need to protect from blood spatter. There were no worries of ickiness with two in the back of the head with a .22 caliber. The weight of the gun in the pocket of his jacket made him feel relaxed and comfortable.

The whole frame job thing, it was a good idea in concept, but had been a disaster in practice. He was a loner, that's one of the things that made him such a good hitter. Working with someone else, especially some psycho amateur, had been stressful. Worse yet, the convoluted schemes the writer came up with in his little frame shop were a lot of effort and generated a lot of anxiety.

Better to do what he was good at, what had never gotten him caught. Better to do it right. Not that he hadn't learned a thing or two from his exasperating experiences with the amateur co-conspirator and professional dickwad.

#

Guy felt an unexpected glow of warm contentment as he located the NID outside of Sweater Vest's house and hung in the bushes, watching his quarry.

Old times. Good times.

He glanced at his watch as he surveilled Sweater Vest, who he now knew from a plaque on the mailbox to be Harold J. Ackerman. Sweater Vest was grimacing and wincing as he made marks on a short stack of papers, like maybe he was grading essay question responses or term papers. Funny, Guy wouldn't have guessed—he was way too smart to create an electronic trail by Googling for definitive info—that Sweater Vest was a teacher. Quite frankly, Guy didn't think his soon-to-be-erstwhile partner had the temperament or smarts to be teaching impressionable youth.

Jeez, he had hoped the guy would be toddling off to bed after playing a first-person-shooter video game or something, not settling in for a long haul of marking up papers. His other appointment tonight was on a tight schedule.

Well, if Sweater Vest had done one thing, it was to make Guy more comfortable going outside of his comfort zone. He unplugged the phone line, pressed the button on a new device he'd brought in his left pants pocket, and stepped out of the bushes, walking around to the front door.

He rang the doorbell.

Ding, dong. Hit man calling.

He feigned a bored, casual expression, just in case Sweater Vest looked out the peephole before answering, but he needn't have bothered. Like most guys, Sweater Vest simply opened the door to see who was outside.

Men didn't worry about being attacked 24/7. Gals, they were almost always more alert, for good reason, sad to say.

As the door opened, Guy dialed up a quick smile and casually moved his right foot forward as a subtle block in case Sweater Vest should try to close the door.

"Jesus!" exclaimed Sweater Vest. "What are you doing here?" His eyes flicked toward a grandfather's clock on one side of the entryway. "How'd you ... Shouldn't you be ..."

"Relax, partner," he replied, doing his best to make his voice soothing. "Just had a quick question, but I'd prefer not to stand here, where all of your neighbors can see, while we chat."

Sweater Vest's eyes, already wide, now scanned back and forth to either side of Guy, looking down the street. "Yeah. I mean, sure." He backed up and swung the door wide.

Guy stepped in, moving well into the entryway and closing the door behind him. "Sorry to intrude, but when I realized you were in the neighborhood and I needed a bit of a refresher on the plan, I figured I'd just stop by and ask."

Sweater Vest backed into the living room, his hands fidgeting and his eyes still wide. "But, how'd you know I was in the neighborhood?"

Guy threw him a shrug and fluttered his right hand, before casually putting it in the pocket of the light jacket he was wearing. "Harold, I'm a professional. You don't think I do a little background research on my professional colleagues?"

"Oh," replied Sweater Vest. "I guess that makes sense." He finally stopped backing away and folded his arms across his chest. "So, you needed a refresher? Wasn't everything in the plotline I wrote up for you?"

Guy tilted his head to one side and wrinkled his nose. "Sure, but I always destroy those sheets before the, you know, the actual job. Just bein' careful and all." He looked down, doing his best to act sheepish. "But as I was driving out here, all of a sudden I realized I couldn't remember the name of the fellow you wanted me to frame up. Begins with a 'B-R' I know, but I know it's not Bruce, cuz you were real emphatic about that, but all I can think of is 'Brian' and us talking about whether that was with an 'I' or a 'Y,' but that didn't seem right ..."

"Bryce. It's Bryce, with a 'Y,'" Sweater Vest snapped. "The person you are setting up is named Bryce."

Guy shook his head. "No. No, that doesn't sound right."

Sweater Vest furrowed his brow and his arms fell out of their folded position, dropping to his sides. "What do you mean, 'that doesn't sound right'? I should know, I'm the one in charge of this frame job ..."

It only took an instant for the .22 revolver to clear Guy's jacket pocket. He strode forward, pushing it up to eye level, scant inches from Sweater Vest's face.

Sweater Vest uttered a choked "Eeep," as the gun barrel appeared before his face, but didn't bolt. Instead he merely opened his palms and raised his arms straight out, at an acute angle from his body. "You," the kid blurted out, with only a small crack in his voice, "you are, of course, in charge of the job. I just provide details for the frame. No offense intended."

"But I do take offense when people try to stiff me for a job."

Sweater Vest's eyebrows tilted inward. "I ... what? I don't understand."

Guy motioned with his head as he talked and Sweater Vest took his meaning, slowly backing to the easy chair in front of the television and, with another head tilt from Guy, sitting down. "Oh, c'mon," said Guy, "it doesn't take a rocket surgeon to figure this out. There's a job in your neck of the woods and you are adamant that a specific person gets tagged with the frame. Cell phone video, plus specific initials in blood, blah, blah, blah. You want this guy to go down and you want it real bad. You'd order a hit on poor Bryce, but you're cheap and you figure you can use me to frame the guy, to do your dirty work, without having to pay."

Sweater Vest's eyes barely left the barrel of the gun, flicking up toward Guy's face only fleetingly, as Guy moved toward the chair.

"Hey," Guy continued. "I don't mind doing a favor for a friend. But, I do, you know, like the courtesy of being asked."

"Sure," agreed Sweater Vest with an exaggerated nod of his head. "My bad. My ... uh ... social skills aren't really what they should be."

"Y'think?"

"Sorry for overstepping. I'd appreciate it if you could, you know, do me this favor in connection with ... uh ... our current project, if it wouldn't inconvenience you."

Guy barked out a laugh. "Inconvenience is what I'm all about, but I get your drift. There's just one other thing, though."

"Sure, sure. What's that?"

"If I do a favor for someone, especially a favor this big, I need to make sure they've got the balls to see it through. Can't have them feeling guilty and giving me up or shit like that."

Sweater Vest's words came out in a rush, the strain of the situation revealing itself as his voice continued to crack. "No problem there. I've got your back. I'm tougher than I look."

"I believe you, not that you look so tough," said Guy nodding, as he backed a bit away from the chair, slowly drifting a few steps back, but still centered in front of the Lay-Z-Boy. "At the very least, I believe *you* think you're a real big-time tough guy. But I've got a little test that will give me some assurance both as to your *bona fides* and your *cajonés*." He reached with his left hand into the small of his back, to the waistband under his jacket, and pulled out another, larger gun. He glanced down at it for just a second. "This here is a .38 revolver, loaded with hollow-tip bullets. It can put a hole in you and come out the back with enough force and spread to blow out the padding and springs of your recliner, leaving a bloody, dinner-plate sized void that can't never be re-upholstered. And, yeah, I can fire left-handed with no difficulty hitting you, especially at this range."

"Okay," whispered Sweater Vest, his forehead beginning to glisten with sweat.

"So here's what we're going to do." He bobbed his right hand, holding the .22. "This is an IOF .22 caliber revolver. It holds up to eight rounds. I'm going to give you this gun. Maybe it's loaded, maybe it's not. Maybe it's got a single bullet or two bullets or four. You don't have a fucking clue. And while I stand here watching, you're going to show me how tough you really are by putting that gun in your mouth and pulling the trigger."

"I am?"

"You are. Either that or I shoot you with the .38 as you sit there."

Guy watched as Sweater Vest pursed his lips, clearly running through the various scenarios in his mind.

"That's okay," Guy chided. "Think it through if you want. I admit, I'd be more impressed if you just took the gun and quickly did as asked, but a deliberate man can still be a tough man." He paused for a moment before continuing. "Let me help you out, because that's what partners are for. Right? First off, you're wondering if you'll be able to tell if the gun is loaded from the heft. But I don't think you've handled many guns, certainly not any Indian made, eight round .22s, so that's not really going to be much help. Instead, you're analyzing the logical dynamics of the situation. The first thought that crosses your mind is that I'd be an idiot to hand you a fully loaded gun ... or even a partially loaded gun with a bullet about to fire ... because you could just take it and shoot me.

"Of course, you're an amateur with guns. You may not even know whether the safety is on or off. And I'm sitting here with a .38 loaded with dum-dums aimed at your chest, so I could be confident that I'm at no risk." He grinned and shrugged. "Still, even a newbie can get off a lucky shot and you've seen from our time together that I'm pretty compulsive about minimizing unnecessary risks.

"And even though you worry a bit that I might be pissed off because you asked for a bigger cut at our last meet, you know if I really wanted you dead, you'd already be dead, and none the wiser, so this probably is some bullshit hitter initiation crap or tough guy test. So you're hoping that you can just take the gun, put it in your mouth, and nonchalantly pull the trigger without your hand shaking too much or, worse yet, pissing your pants. Then you'll be able to go forward from our encounter—not only with our arrangement, but with your life— knowing, actually *knowing*, that you are a big, bad MoFo with balls of fucking steel and that you and I, we are solid for life. One simple act can change you forever, make you the man you always wanted to be."

Guy took a step forward and placed the .22 on Sweater Vest's still thankfully dry lap. He stepped well back from the chair, keeping the .38 steady on his colleague's chest. "This is your chance, Harold. Forget about your daydreams and make-believe stories. Join the real world. Be a fucking man."

Sweater Vest looked at the gun for a moment, his tongue peeking out from his closed mouth for just an instant. Then he picked up the weapon, hefted it in his hands, and grabbed the grip with his right hand. He pointed it at himself, using his left hand to steady and guide the weapon into his open mouth, in and up. He shut his eyes tight and slowly began to squeeze the trigger.

Chapter 18

Bryce and Gantry sat in the darkness of Christoph's place, waiting.

"Tell me again," complained Bryce, "why we just can't call the police now?"

Gantry exhaled with a huff. The responsibility for the plan pressed down on him more heavily than the smothering blackness of the setting. "Because we don't know if the hit man is connected or routinely scans the police radio frequencies. Once he's here, once he's committed, we make the call."

"Yeah," muttered Bryce. "Don't worry about that part. My thumbs are already hovering over the speed-dial key and we're not expecting anyone to show up for almost an hour and a half."

Gantry nodded his head at his fellow writer. "So, we're ready, then. What's the worry?"

Bryce snorted a laugh. "What's the worry? Maybe the worry is that a professional hit man who, according to your sources, has an impeccable record for job-related effectiveness, is going to creep up with lethal intent to the empty house we are hiding in and our main defenses are, one, that the guy he's looking for isn't actually here and, two, that AT&T has dependable cell phone coverage. What're we going to do during the four to twelve minutes it takes for the police to get here? Play charades?" He shook his head. "Let me get a head start ..." He held up three fingers, then one, then made air quotes with just one hand and again flashed three fingers, continuing to speak during his show and tell: "Three words. First word. Repeated three times." He put his thumb up and his pointing finger out in the traditional pantomime for a gun, then pressed his finger against his temple and jerked his head to the side simultaneously with jerking his pointing finger skyward, repeating the routine three times. "Dead. Dead. Dead."

"What's with the single air quotes?"

Bryce's eyes flicked toward heaven. "That's your take-away? 'What's with the single air quotes?'" He used his right hand to rub at his temples. "They were ditto marks. You support Hack's ridiculous octothorpe rant and you don't recognize ditto marks?" His shoulders slumped forward. "Glad to know I could pass on some useful wisdom before I die. Tell me, Mrs. Lincoln, other than the gruesome death of The President, did you at least enjoy the show?"

Gantry pursed his lips for a moment before responding. "I found it overly dramatic and unrealistic."

"Unrealistic?"

"Perhaps a better phrase would be 'a doubtful prognostication of the evening's likely events.'"

"Really."

Gantry looked his friend in the eye. "Sure, there's some risk in this plan, but we've minimized it. According to the scenario we fed to Harold, the hit man won't be using a gun, so he probably won't even be packing. Just makes him more suspicious should he be seen or stopped. He's supposed to use a blunt weapon available on scene, so he may not be armed at all. Since the first thing we did when we got here was to remove and sequester all handy makeshift weapons, there's no bat or trophy or guitar or fireplace poker to grab to strike us. All he'll probably have is his fists, maybe a pocket knife."

Bryce nodded. "Okay, good. So, I've got nothing to worry about, except maybe getting beaten and stabbed to death."

"That's why we're wearing heavy clothing, despite the warm weather. Doubtful even a tough guy could beat us to death before the cops would arrive."

"Ahhh, pain and permanent injury, the happy alternative to death."

"Look," said Gantry, "there's some risk, sure. But we have a good plan and noble intentions. Everything will work out in the end."

"That's what the North thought when the Civil War started."

"So? They were right, weren't they?"

"Oh, yeah. They were right. It's just the half-a-million dead and years of pain and misery that makes it a parallel that's not so comforting right now."

Gantry laughed.

"What's so damn funny?" Bryce demanded.

"You just reminded me of a Danger McAdams line."

"What's that?"

"If you want a comfortable life, don't get in the way of bad guys for a living ... or for a dame."

#

Blam!

Sweater Vest's head jerked backward as his body slumped forward, gunsmoke roiling out of his mouth just ahead of a small torrent of blood from the gunshot wound. At that angle, the bullet would have torn through the roof of Sweater Vest's mouth, through the sinus cavity, and into the brain. Although blood drained out of the entrance wound from either corner of Sweater Vest's mouth, the splatter from the shot had been minimal. Guy looked down for a moment, confirming he had been far enough back to be clear of any obvious blood contamination. Nothing he could see, but he'd burn his clothes at his fishing cabin later, just like he always did. His standard routine reflected a high degree of care and paranoia. After all, that Luminol crap the crime scene jockeys used could trigger off of nothing more than residue from the mist of microscopic blood droplets lingering in the air after a hit.

Meanwhile, just to be sure he didn't create a trail of naked eye evidence, he snagged a pair of paper booties out of his left jacket pocket as he tucked the .38 inside. He slipped the booties on where he stood, then circled the body at a distance, confirming that there was no exit wound, that the bullet had bounced around inside Sweater Vest's skull, erasing not only him, but any evidence of his memories or interactions with Guy.

He did not approach or disturb the body. Suburban police departments were crap at murder investigations, but nothing he could do could possibly improve the realism of the suicide from a forensics standpoint. Gunshot residue would clearly show that Sweater Vest held the gun to his own open mouth when pulling the trigger. No bruise marks on his mouth to indicate the gun was forced inside; no voids in the GSR to suggest someone had been holding his hands. No signs of a struggle; no forced entry.

Guy quickly walked over to the modern, programmable thermostat— houses this new always had the modern kind—and worked for a few minutes, setting it so the heat would come on, heating the place to a toasty 87° Fahrenheit for the night, then turning on the air conditioning come dawn's early light. When and if the county medical examiner checked liver temp to determine time of death, after consulting a chart which tracked liver cooling characteristics to ambient temperature, the earlier heat would throw off calculations just enough that it would look like Sweater Vest had offed himself a few hours after he actually had. Just long enough that the presumed time of death would be after another death by .22 that was scheduled to occur in just a bit more than an hour, using another gun currently tucked into Guy's glove compartment.

He didn't worry about the rifling on the bullets creating a ballistics mismatch.   A .22 to the head created so much deformation, fragmentation, and damage that .22 bullets, especially lead ones, were rarely even run for ballistic matches. And, since the two weapons were of the same make, manufacture, and age, the gross characteristics, like direction of the twist, would, if visible, be consistent.

Besides, Guy didn't really care that much if the cops thought Sweater Vest offed himself because of crushing guilt of committing a murder earlier in the night or because he was a lonely loser. Dead was dead.

Guy wouldn't be attending the funeral.

He paused just a moment at the door to look back and take in the scene.

Holy mother of God, Guy had convinced the dipshit not only to kill himself, but to frame himself for tonight's second act.

He didn't need Sweater Vest any more.

He was his own fucking frame shop.

Chapter 19

"Psssst!" hissed Bryce, causing Gantry to jerk in surprise. This was the reason Gantry had Danger McAdams work alone. "I hear somebody coming."

"Then shut the fuck up," growled Gantry.

"But, he's almost half an hour early."

"So? Stick to the plan. Dial the cops."

Gantry watched out of one corner of his eye at Bryce, crouching behind the table in the adjoining dining room. The epic poet fidgeted with his phone, first simply pressing his thumb against the screen, then frantically jabbing it repeatedly with his index finger. "Noooooo. Shit! Shit! Shit!"

"Shut the fuck up!"

Bryce glared at him, his eyes wide. "There's no signal! I can't get through to the police."

Fuck. Things were not going according to plan. "Well, then, I guess we'll just have to ..."

Gantry stopped talking as he heard the faint rattle of the front door knob. The hit man was obviously picking the lock. Gantry hunkered down behind the sofa, peeking out from near the corner of an oversized throw pillow over-topping the back of the sofa at one end. Only a few seconds later, he saw the knob turn and the door ease open. A bulky, looming shadow pressed close against the opening door, still blocking most of the ambient light of the widely spaced, old-fashioned streetlights outside from filtering in. The dark figure stepped adroitly to the side and used his left hand to slowly press the door shut behind him, but just as he did, the dim light from the street glinted off of an unmistakable shape in the hit man's right hand.

A gun.

Despite all their plans. Despite the plot they had practically forced down Harold's throat, the hit man had a gun. Worse yet, he was leading with it.

A sharp intake of breath from the right confirmed Bryce had seen it, too. He could only pray that the soft click of the door latching shut behind the hit man had masked the sound. He flicked his eyes toward Bryce, hoping to catch his attention and motion for him to be quiet, then bit his own lip, drawing blood, to keep himself from vocalizing the expletives that overpowered his mind.

The screen from Bryce's cell phone glowed from behind the dining room table, as Bryce continued to jab at it.

As a thriller writer, he recognized the scenario. Once things started going bad, they got worse and worse, until finally someone died or did something incredibly brave and stupid to stop things from spiraling all the way down the crapper.

If he were Danger McAdams, what would he do? Well, he'd probably shoot the bad guy with the .45 in his jacket pocket, then smoke a cigarette while he waited for the cops to come arrest him. Except, Gantry wasn't a private eye, didn't own a .45, and had never smoked in his life.

So much for fiction coming to life.

Instead, he used his right hand to make a cutting motion across his own throat—praying the motion didn't end up being eerily prophetic—in the hope Bryce would see it and power down or flip over his phone to eliminate the colorful tell-tale glow. At the same time, he reached into his left pocket with his other hand and fingered on his own cell phone.

Maybe he could get a signal where Bryce had failed.

If not, he was going to have a serious talk with Verizon about their maps, assuming he survived the night.

He waited, interminably it seemed, for the cell phone start-up to complete. When he could perceive a faint glow through the fabric of his slacks, he pulled out the phone, screen angled down and away from the door, and thumbed the screen to the phone function, dialing 9-1-1 as quickly as he could in the awkward position.

A few seconds later, the screen of death flashed on. No signal.

Fuck.

Then things got worse.

"You," a voice barked out, "behind the couch. I know you're there. Stand up, with your hands in clear sight."

What would Danger McAdams do now, if he was as ill-prepared as Gantry was? Something incredibly brave and stupid. What could Gantry, a genteel writer, do? He could only do what writers do.

He decided to banter.

He thumbed the phone to its home screen as he stood slowly, his hands palms out at either side.

Those who can't, don't teach. They bluff.

"Chrisoph's not here," he announced as he stood. "You've been set up." He nodded toward his phone. "The cops are on their way."

The hit man sneered at him. "Really? That's your play? Piss off the guy with the gun by telling him you set him up and then lie about having back-up?" He chuckled. "Even Sweater Vest wouldn't write such a lame plot."

Sweater Vest? Probably the guy's nickname for Harold. Hoods and low-lifes had a fondness for avoiding real names.

"What makes you think I'm lying?"

The hit man reached into his pants pocket with his left hand, and pulled out a thick electronic device the size cell phones used to be. "Cell signal jammer. Got it online. Movie theaters use 'em. Libraries, too. Some churches. Avoids interruptions." He grinned as he put it back in his pocket. "Used to be, cutting of the landline was enough, but you gotta change with the times."

Gantry did his best to play it cool. He kept his face blank, as if unimpressed.

"They do a good job on 4G," he lied. "But my phone's an older model. I'd suggest you ask for a refund, but most online sellers won't allow return of electronics and you don't get much internet time in the big house."

He continued to play his bad hand, stalling for God knows what. Maybe Bryce could escape out the kitchen door and run to the neighbor's for help. Let's see, getting a sleeping neighbor to wake up to pounding at the door in the middle of the night and call the cops. Hell, he'd better steer the conversation to sex, politics, or religion, 'cause there was no way he could stretch out chatting about cell coverage and warranties for twenty minutes.

"So, how long has Harold been manufacturing frames for you? He's not really that strong of a mystery writer, you know." He forced a chuckle. "I hear a cat figured out one of his crimes."

The hit man's brow furrowed at Gantry's last comment, but, unfortunately the guy didn't take the bait. "You're stalling for time. Where's Christoph?"

Gantry shrugged. "I already told you, not here. He's on tour with his lame-ass band somewhere, from what I understand. You were set up, remember?"

Click.

Gantry prayed that was the faint sound of the kitchen door closing. Now, if he could just keep the hit man calm and talking ...

"What the fuck was that?" Gantry's tormentor asked. "Is there somebody else in the house?"

"Nobody," Gantry responded quickly. "Nobody's here but you and me." He fervently hoped he was telling the truth.

The hit man gave him a broad smile and shook his head, stepping forward from the wall and turning fully toward Gantry, his back to the living room's picture window. "No witnesses, then." He shook his head. "Never admit there are no witnesses."

The hit man held the gun out, raising it to eye level, no doubt improving his ability to aim. Nothing quite so dramatic as cocking the gun, but Gantry knew those scenes were not only cliché, they were lies. Modern weapons generally don't require cocking. And if you are pointing a gun which requires cocking at someone without cocking it, you are either an idiot or the character in a bad mystery thriller.

Gantry tensed to jump, like a World Cup goalie on a penalty kick. Not only did he have to guess where to leap, but he had to time it right or his opponent would see the move and adjust, accordingly.

There was a flash of light, bright in the darkness, and the deafening roar of an explosion accompanied by a crash of glass and a rush of air. A sharp, slicing pain torn through the outside of Gantry's left thigh as he simultaneously leapt to the right. He landed on the floor with a heavy thud as the jolt of pain shot up his leg again, with even greater insistence. He ignored the pain and scrambled up and back, hot jolts exploding through his leg as he stampeded through the dining room crouched low, as oblivious to the racket he was making as a deaf-mute commando. His frantic rush sent chairs askitter as he crashed toward the kitchen door, waiting for the inevitable second bullet to hit him in the back, paralyzing him, forcing him to watch as the third was sent point blank into his head.

He threw open the door and was immediately thrown to the ground by a shadowy figure rushing into the house. He fell back onto his left side and his leg burned once more with stabbing pain. He and his assailant rolled and wrestled, grabbing and punching ineffectively in the close quarters, doing more damage from colliding with appliances and cabinets than with their fists, until suddenly his opponent cried out: "Gantry?"

"Bryce?"

And then the kitchen lights came on and they both froze.

Gantry was on the bottom of the pile-up at the moment, sighting along the linoleum floor as two dark, heavy shoes moved tentatively into the kitchen. Gantry flicked his eyes across the floor, hoping against hope his bizarre struggle with Bryce had knocked a large, kitchen knife or rolling pin or some other useable weapon to the floor. But, no. There was no chance of that. Bryce and he had carefully removed all potential weapons from the house in preparation for accosting their supposedly weaponless hit man and holding him until the police arrived.

He looked again at the dark shoes, wondering if they would be the last thing he ever saw.

This was the end of Gantry Ellis. This was the end of Danger McAdams.

Dark shoes.

Dark orthopedic shoes.

What the fuck? Were those white socks? Was that the rubber tip of a cane nearby?

"If you two are through playing grab-ass on the kitchen floor," said a familiar voice, "you might want to get up so we can get the hell out of Dodge."

It couldn't be. Could it?

Bryce rolled off of him and the two of them stood up shakily.

Although his head was far from clear and his eyes were still adjusting to the bright fluorescent lights glinting off of the genuine Formica countertop, Gantry looked toward the doorway to the dining room and saw the nonagenarian body of Sergeant Carl Pilkington holding, in his slightly trembling right hand, the oddest looking gun he had ever seen.

"For one thing," said the old gent, "I have to get rid of this goddamn gun before I get caught with it." He winked at Gantry. "We weren't supposed to take war souvenirs—too many supposedly discarded guns were booby-trapped. Besides, it'll be damn hard to keep it hidden once I move into Pine Meadows Assisted Living Facility next month."

Bryce expressed Gantry's exact thoughts with elegance.

"But, what? How'd you ...? Huh? What the fuck?"

The old man shrugged. "Overheard you two talking after the last group session. Y'know, the one where you two fed Harold the convoluted murder for hire by someone protecting a lady who was getting beat up? I move kinda slow, so I hung back a bit, thinking you two might be thinking of doing something stupid and highly illegal to protect Minx, poor thing. I'm feeble, though, not deaf. Heard the whole stupid plan about putting out a fake hit through your contacts, Gantry, to catch the professional assassin you surmised Harold was working with." Carl shook his head. "Harold was always pretty desperate for an audience, any audience."

Bryce scrunched up his face. "But, you never said anything."

"Nobody listens to old men, but great-grandkids." He shrugged again. "Figured you wouldn't listen to reason, but thought you might need some back-up."

Carl hefted the weapon as he continued. "Nazi Luger. Cleaned her, but wasn't sure the cartridges would still fire. Semi-automatic, but given the recoil and my age, figured I'd do best to aim well with the first shot."

"You got the hit man?" asked Bryce, his eyes flicking past the Sergeant, toward the living room. "Are you sure he's down for good?"

Carl's nose twitched. "I've seen dead before. He's dead."

"Then, who shot me?" asked Gantry, as he looked down at his leg. A sharp spike of glass protruded from the outer side of his left thigh. Surprisingly, there was almost no blood.

"It's a shard of glass," said Bryce.

"Single pane glass window," said Carl. "None of that modern, safety glass. No match for a nine millimeter round. Sorry it blew back the glass far enough to get you when I fired from the porch."

Gantry smiled. "I'll live."

Carl winked. "That was the point."

Epilogue

They never did call the police. Carl had insisted he didn't want to spend his last few years explaining himself when his conscience was perfectly clear.

Gantry finally relented. Bryce went along. Gantry figured it was because even though Bryce had returned to the house when he thought Gantry was shot, Bryce didn't think that unsuccessfully trying to call 9-1-1 repeatedly before running out the back door was a tale likely to impress the ladies.

With no bloodstains from Gantry's injury and an unregistered, untraceable Nazi-era weapon, a thorough wipe-down of fingerprints was all it took to baffle the local cops, who were overburdened with an unrelated suicide across town, and who had no clue why a burglar who broke into an empty house was blown away from outside the house with an antique weapon.

Oh, sure, they questioned the clueless neighbors and even Christoph, who was performing with his band more than a thousand miles away, in Boulder, Colorado, at the time of the crime, but the case went cold quick.

And that was just fine with Gantry, who vowed to always do his own interviews with bad guys in the future.

Gantry, Bryce, and Carl had, of course, been surprised by the death of Harold, but not particularly broken up about it. The serendipitous tying up of loose ends was simplifying. Besides, Hack had proved himself to be a bad guy, not just a bad writer, and goodness knows the world had enough of both.

Myrtle and Felicity sobbed heartily at Harold's funeral. Gantry noticed even Minx shed a tear. Carl sat during the graveside service, while the others stood. It was a small affair. Most tossed handwritten poems into the grave as they passed by. Gantry dropped in an autographed Danger McAdams mystery. Bryce tossed in a small sheaf of papers; Gantry wasn't sure, but it looked like it might be a mark-up of one of Harold's stories.

Afterwards, as Bryce and Gantry walked alone together through the cemetery, toward their cars, Bryce put his hand on Gantry's shoulder and stopped him for a moment.

"Thanks," said Bryce, his voice quiet, but firm. "Thanks, for standing up to that hit man when I screwed up."

Gantry gave him a wan smile. "You didn't screw up. It was my plan; my responsibility. Nobody figured on a cell phone jammer."

"So, I guess you've got plenty of material out of all this for your next Danger McAdams mystery, at least."

Gantry wrinkled his nose and shook his head. "Nah. Writing fiction about writing and writers is self-absorbed enough. Writing fiction based on actual fact about writing and writers is just too cliché and too self-aggrandizing for me. Not too smart if we want to maintain our low profile, anyhow, and I think we both, you and me, owe that much and more to Carl."

"That's the truth," agreed Bryce.

"Besides, I think I'll set aside Danger McAdams for a while. Try something new."

Bryce's eyes narrowed. "I don't have to worry about a new name in epic Civil War poetry, do I?"

"Nah," said Gantry, as he started walking again. "I thought maybe I'd try a genuine, novel-length cat mystery. Doesn't seem like anyone has ever done that genre proud."

Bryce laughed. "Certainly not Hack ..."

The End

Addendum

EYE WITNESS

A cat mystery by Harold J. Ackerman

"You saw this yourself?" Shamus McGee stroked his whiskers absentmindedly as he peered at Willie, sizing him up. Willie was usually reliable, but he hadn't seen head or tail of the snitch for some months now and things can happen——things that can cause once trustworthy sources to become untrustworthy, even dangerous. The reasons were many: hard times; narcotics; mental illness; religious fervor; old age. He'd seen them all in his decades as a private investigator and he had to be sure of his information. This was a wild, wild tale——the kind that folks talk about in gatherings on Saturday night or when they meet up during a Sunday walk in the park. His reputation was on the line if he reported to the client that this was actually the solution to the mystery. He wanted to be sure he got it right.

"Absolutely, Shamus. Without a doubt. I mean, I couldn't believe my eyes at first, but when you think about it, it explains everything ... well, almost everything." Willie twitched with excitement, or perhaps worry, about the information he had just imparted. Shamus couldn't be sure which yet and he needed to know.

Willie's tale was a blockbuster, if true. The religious establishment was bound to be apoplectic. Willie would be investigated and denounced at the very least. His name, his history, everything about him would be sniffed out, batted about to see what shook loose, then released to the news-mongering horde in a manner calculated to make sure their frenzied attacks and yowls of protest lasted as long as possible.

Shamus would be unlikely to fare much better, but at least he had a long professional reputation and some friends, or at least long-established contacts, in the news dissemination business. They would hold off on him for a while. Long enough to see how the basic story sold and whether his bizarre explanation of the ultimate mystery was going to win the day. Then, if it looked like Willie's information was bogus, they would pounce and tear him apart, too.

It was past strange that he had ever even gotten this assignment. He'd been in the detective business a numbingly long time, but he didn't go for the sensational jobs. This, well this was truly sensational and the oddest case he'd ever worked ... by far. Most of the jobs were straightforward enough, if not downright routine. Not always simple work or pleasant either, but what you expected in the business. Staking out houses and tailing suspects, mostly catching those who cheated on their supposed loved-ones. He'd seen too many mates leave home in the evening to go visit some piece of tail than he cared to think about.

The clients wanted to know, but they didn't necessarily want to see what was going on right under their noses—-most of his clients really didn't get out that much and couldn't handle themselves on the streets like he could. Sure, there was some excitement in the job—-an occasional car chase, that kind of thing. But most of the cases were just sad and pathetic.

He hated the missing children cases the worst. Yeah, he had a few successes in his time locating the young ones—some even alive—but there were just too many cases of kids plucked away from their homes or getting lost or just turning up missing to make any sense of the world. The religious just said there was an unknowable reason for everything. The lunatic fringe—-fanatics who caterwaul at the moon—-they all had theories of abduction and such. Heck, their weirdo theories made as much sense as this case—-which reminded him, he'd better get down to business. His client was paying him to track down the secret of the mysterious "manna," not daydream about his crummy job.

"Let's go over the entire story, Willie."

"Geez, Shamus, I've already told you I saw the whole thing!"

"But I've got to make sure what you saw makes sense. I can't just take your word for it. You know, there's no bonus for you and no future work from me, not next week, not in a blue moon, if you screw up something this important. Heck, you'll be lucky to eat out of a garbage can if word gets about that you lied ..."

"Lied! You know me, Shamus, I ain't no liar!" Willie's nervous twitch became more pronounced.

"... or were mistaken about what you saw. You say it all happened in Seattle? That's some distance away. What were you doing there?"

"What does it matter?" Willie's gaze went to the side, then down, looking anywhere but in Shamus' eyes.

"A good detective corroborates every part of the informant's story he can."

"It's embarrassing ..."

Shamus opened his mouth in anger, but withheld some of the fury of his words: "So is telling a tale like this and not being able to prove it! What were you doing in Seattle? I need to know and I need to know

now. It doesn't help either of us if the first time I hear about it is on the evening news."

"I followed a girl there."

Shamus considered this for a moment. Willie wasn't exactly a catch, but some of the city dames are pretty randy. Of course, the consequences of casual promiscuity were anything but casual. That's one of the reasons there were so many unwanted offspring in the world. He focused back on the questioning. "Does she know you were there or were you stalking her from a distance?"

"I wouldn't call it stalking ... anyway, whatever you call it, she knew I was there. She caught me ... I mean, saw me."

"What's her name?"

"Muffy."

"Geez, Willie, you know those rich suburban types will never go for a cat like you!" Shamus thought for a few seconds, unconsciously humming a monotonous tune. "Let's go back to the mystery, itself, and make sure we have all the appropriate elements."

"Whatever. You're the detective, Shamus."

"Alright. Now in most of the world, everyone fends for themselves. They work for their food each and every day. But then, well, then there's the rich—-they live in fancy houses, people tend to their every need, and their meals are served to them on silver platters. My task is to find the source of their bounty. There's no ready evidence of where it all comes from. No one sees it, no one smells it. It sure doesn't walk into the place by itself."

"Wouldn't that be the cat's meow?"

"Yet every day, the servants of the rich take this cylindrical object, subject it to some mechanical purring apparatus, then, there it is ... food on a silver platter. The priests call it "manna from heaven.""

"That's the story."

"The priests also say that the servants of the pure of soul pray for provisions. If their prayers are answered, the gods purr and immediately thereafter food mysteriously appears from nowhere, provided to these rich cats because they are the chosen ones. But you say that's not what really happens."

"Never happened to me, boss, one way or the other, but this Muffy ... I saw it happen to her when I was stalking ... er ... watching her. It made me real jealous ... and hungry, too. So I got pissed and left. Thought I'd head down to the waterfront and see what I could catch to eat. That's when I saw it. Big place, huge place. I could barely believe it, Shamus. Filled with the best food you ever smelled. Big old boats were coming in filled with fish and stuff and they were chopping it up and putting it into these cylindrical objects, then sealing them real tight—-not like a garbage can lid, boss—-I mean, real tight so you couldn't even smell the food was in 'em.

"They called it a cannery. Cans is what they called the cylindrical objects. Trucks full of the stuff were leaving for all sorts of places. I followed one and it went to a big building where there were lots of these cans and some regular food, too. Servants would saunter in and bring the cans home. That's why you can't see or smell the food coming in— it's sealed real tight. I got one of them cans and no matter what I did, I couldn't get it open."

"So you're asking me to believe that the servants have created an entire workforce dedicated to catching food and shipping it hundreds of miles to other servants, who magically unseal it and feed it to us."

"That's about it."

This was just too much. Willie had told him earlier that the food was inside the strange cylindrical objects, but he hadn't told him this whole fantastic story about hordes of servants conspiring to make it appear. He could no longer control his disbelief of the entire story. Shamus spat out his words: "But it makes no sense, Willie. Food doesn't keep long enough to travel hundreds of miles. And besides, why would they do that? What's the purring sound? I just can't stake my professional reputation on an explanation so outlandish! I'll be labeled a heretic, for cat's sake."

"But it's true!"

"Sure, sure, Willie. I suppose next you're going to explain the mysterious red lights that have been reported lately, moving erratically at incredible speeds with no sound or source of power."

"Well, a cat in Seattle named MicroSoftie was telling me about something called 'laser pointers' ..."

That did it. Shamus arched his back and hissed. Willie leapt from the top of the park bench and skittered away through a hole in the fence. "Laser pointer, my tail!" he fumed. "Next thing you know, he'll be trying to convince me that the servants are the chosen ones ..."

Acknowledgments

Even though writing is usually a lonely business, there are lots of people who have a hand in conducting a Kickstarter project and getting a finished book out to the public. Their contributions are as varied as are their personalities and I wish to thank them all, including: TS Rhodes, Janine K. Spendlove, Bruce Steinberg (aka BR Robb), J.E. Mooney, Buck Hanno, and Jean Rabe, for offering stories, novellas, and books as stretch goals for the Kickstarter (you should buy their stuff); Hal Walker, for advising me about a few forensics and law enforcement matters; Randy Martin, for encouragement, enthusiasm, and tremendous technical help in getting the audio for my Kickstarter to actually sound like me; Lori Linehan Swan, for teaching me the word "octothorpe" during a game of *Password*; Steven Saus and Rich Bingle, for assisting with technical matters regarding fulfillment; Bruce Steinberg, for blurbing the book and providing editing and story suggestions (he is responsible for the apostrophes facing the correct direction in shortened words); Jenn Brozek and Janine K. Spendlove, for letting me guest blog on their sites during the Kickstarter; Anne Veague and Kevin Moriarity, for allowing me to read from my book at Waterline Writers and for rushing the video to help with fundraising; Jean Rabe, for generally being the best friend a writer could ever have; Chris Verstraete, for assistance with a synopsis and some comments on the prologue; my writing pals in the Gen Con Writer's Symposium, Origins Game Fair Library, and St. Charles Writers' Group, for putting up with me (and, in the case of the SCWG, critiquing a few key scenes of my story); all of my friends, family members, acquaintances, writing pals, and participants in various

Facebook, Twitter, and other online groups, including a number of crazy participants in GISHWHES (the Greatest International Scavenger Hunt the World Has Ever Seen), for spreading the word about my little project; and Linda M. Bingle, for editing contributions, support, encouragement, and general awesomeness.

By the way, I actually wrote "Eye Witness" many, many years ago and submitted it to the anthology of one hundred cat mysteries Barnes & Noble was then putting together. It was rejected for that project, but eventually found its way to print nine years later in *Catopolis*, edited by Martin H. Greenberg and Janet Deaver-Pack (DAW Books; 2008). I thought it would be amusing to have the PMWGCS critique a real story based on some misgivings I had about the story after I got some distance from it. Despite that touch of reality and what I am sure will be a lot of speculation by some of my writer pals about who various characters are based upon, please understand that *Frame Shop* is a work of fiction and that any resemblance to actual persons, places, and events is not intentional and certainly not meant to be disparaging in any way. Simply put, if you think any of these characters are you or other actual people, that probably says more about you, than it does about me.

Finally, my heartfelt thanks to all of you who backed the Kickstarter project for this book (names rendered per your survey responses): Danielle Ackley-McPhail; Taylor Alcantar; Maggie Allen; Robin Allen; Roberta Asher; Lee Baker; Mike Balcom-Vetillo; Cathy Kern Betts; Bill; James and Marjorie Bingle; Richard and Karen Bingle; Dylan Birtolo; John Bitner; Jill E. Bliss; Darwin Bromley; Doug Burman; Drew Caldwell; Lynn Caldwell; Cynthia Calongne; Thomas Carey; D-Rock; Duncan Dog; The Great and Powerful Maxwell Alexander Drake;

Robert Early; fdj; Fen Eatough; Anonymous Fan; Elaine; Colleen Fasbender; Stuart Fullinwider; Paul Genesse; Richard Graves; Lynne Handy; Sarah Hans; Edward J. Herdrich; Jon Jacobs; Lisa Richelle Jensen; JJ; Scott A. Johnson; Wayne E. Johnson; Vicki Johnson-Steger; Karen and Lee; Mary Konczyk; Helen E. Kourous; Randall Lemon; Don Lindman; madbuzz; Randall Martin; Chanté McCoy; Alice McGee; Rebecca Brewer Mitchell; Daniel Myers; Saad J. Nadhir; Josh and Ashley Peters; Brian Pettera; Vic Polites; Dan Proctor; Chris Bingle Redford; Stephanie Richardson; Roy Romasanta; Adriane Ruzak; David A. Samuels; Steven Saus; Mike Selinker; Silence in the Library Publishing; Tanya Spackman; Janine K. Spendlove; Tom Starr; Bruce Steinberg; Stephen D. Sullivan; Steve; Kelly Swails; Marc Tassin; Eric Quinn Taylor; Mark and Leslie Thomas; Dear Todd – I owe it all to you ... Love and Kisses – Don; Elizabeth Vaughan; Anne Veague; Natalie S. Wainwright; Steve Wales; Craig Walker; Jean Marie Ward; Carolyn R. White; Tim L. White; Betty Wilfong; Gregory A. Wilson; Bryan Young; and Raymond G. Ziemer. You have not only given me confidence that I have an audience out there in the world, but you have demonstrated that self-publishing can pay. Both are incredibly valuable to me as an indie author.

Well, if you've read this far, you either are checking to see if your name was listed in these acknowledgments (in which case, you can go read the book now) or you've just finished the book and are still lingering, laughing, or fuming over it (in which case, please write an honest, thoughtful review and then post it on Amazon). As always, more about me and my writing can be found at http://www.donaldjbingle.com.

Thank you, again.

Aloha,

Don Bingle, November 2014

Please consider writing an honest, thoughtful
review of this publication.

Novels by Donald J. Bingle:

Forced Conversion
GREENSWORD: A Tale of Extreme Global Warming
Net Impact

Stories and Story Collections by Donald J. Bingle

Writer on Demand™ Vol. 1, Tales of Gamers
and Gaming
Writer on Demand™ Vol. 2, Tales of Humorous Horror
Writer on Demand™ Vol. 3, Tales Out of Time
Writer on Demand™ Vol. 4, Grim, Fair e-Tales
Writer on Demand™ Vol. 5, Tales of an Altered Past
Powered by Romance, Horror, and Steam
Writer on Demand™ Vol. 6, Not-So-Heroic Fantasy
Writer on Demand™ Vol. 7, Shadow Realities
Crimson Life/Crimson Death
Season's Critiquings
Gentlemanly Horrors of Mine Alone
Running Free: A Tale Inspired by Patsy Ann
Father's Day Deluxe 3-Pack

Also from 54°40' Orphyte, Inc.

Ratfish by Buck Hanno
Surrounded by Love: A Story of Orphans
and Family by Marjorie L. Bingle

Praise for other books from Donald J. Bingle

Forced Conversion

"Visceral, bloody -- and one hell of a page turner! Bingle tackles the philosophical issues surrounding uploaded consciousness in a fresh, exciting way. This is the debut of a major novelist -- don't miss it."

Robert J. Sawyer, Hugo Award-winning author of <u>Hominids</u>

GREENSWORD

"A novel about three slacker environmentalists may seem an unlikely vehicle for edge-of-the-seat suspense, yet Bingle's satirical eco-terrorist thriller just might haunt readers' nightmares for days."

Booklist

Net Impact

"... a bit of <u>The DaVinci Code</u> with some James Bond and a modern virtual reality spin."

Game Night Reviews

See more at www.donaldjbingle.com